I0551773

One World

The Legend of Draconis

No Longer Legend

in

Book 4

Janet Taylor-Perry

One World

The Legend of Draconis

No Longer Legend

in

Book IV

by

Janet Taylor-Perry

Copyright 2021, Janet Taylor-Perry, all rights reserved. No part of this work may be reproduced, except for brief documented citations, without the author's express consent.

ISBN: 978-0-9990692-9-5

Dragon Breath Press
Ridgeland, Mississippi

Other Books by Janet Taylor-Perry

The Raiford Chronicles:
1. *Lucky Thirteen*—Semifinalist, Faulkner Competition
2. *Heartless*
3. *Broken*—Short list finalist, Faulkner Competition
4. *Whatever It Takes*

The Legend of Draconis:
1. *King Satin's Realm*—Semifinalist, Faulkner Competition
2. *Spirits' Desire*—Winner Preditor and Editor's Award, "other" category
3. *Last of an Exceptional Breed*—Semifinalist, Faulkner Competition

April Chastain Intrigues:
1. *Wilted Magnolias*—Finalist, Faulkner Competition

Laura Beth Copeland Misadventures:
1. *Head Count*—Finalist Faulkner Competition

Hillbilly Hijinks:
1. *Homegrown Healer*—Semifinalist, Faulkner Competition

Gods and Children:
1. *Ain't No Mountain*—Semifinalist, Faulkner Competition

One World

The Legend of Draconis

No Longer Legend

in

Book 4

Janet Taylor-Perry

A Faulkner Wisdom Competition semifinalist

Disclaimer

All entities in this story are purely fictional. Any resemblance to any party, living or dead, is coincidence.

Acknowledgments

Thanks to my plethora of author friends who continually encourage me to practice my craft. Great appreciation to my family for putting up with my eccentricities. Bookoos of gratitude to my editor, mentor, and friend, Lottie Brent Boggan for her no-nonsense approach to keeping me on track. Google her and give her books a read. Gratitude goes to my faithful beta reader, Nidia Hernandez, aka Barbra Best, author of *The Rock Star Records*, fun reads to get lost in. I can never tell Aunt Ruth Ishee how much those telephone read-alouds meant to the growth and development of my art. And no word can express the debt I owe to my fantastic cover designer, Christopher Chambers. Check out his work at juroddesigns.com.

Bookoos—for those who don't know, this is a southern perversion of the French *beaucoup*, meaning a lot, much, many.

Dedication

For Tabitha, Serenity, Annabelle, Gracie, Angelina, Lenylah, Chasity, Alyshia, Victoria, Jada, Charvonna, Kajuan, Audrey, Hawkins, Nicholas, Scout, Matthew, Malachi, Dylan, Jonathan, Shawn, and Justin for making my world awesome. It was a joy and honor to teach you!

I know not with what weapons World War III will be fought, but World War IV will be fought with sticks and stones.

Albert Einstein

So we, being many, are one body in Christ, and every one members one of another.

Romans 12:5

Table of Contents

Prologue

Part Four
Living Legend

This Is My Father's World

This is my Father's world,
and to my listening ears
all nature sings, and round me rings
the music of the spheres.
This is my Father's world:
I rest me in the thought
of rocks and trees, of skies and seas;
his hand the wonders wrought.

This is my Father's world,
the birds their carols raise,
the morning light, the lily white,
declare their maker's praise.
This is my Father's world:
he shines in all that's fair;
in the rustling grass I hear him pass;
he speaks to me everywhere.

This is my Father's world.
O let me ne'er forget
that though the wrong seems oft so strong,
God is the ruler yet.
This is my Father's world:
why should my heart be sad?
The Lord is King; let the heavens ring!
God reigns; let the earth be glad.

℘rologue

Blaring horns screeched in discordant symphony. Screams, wails, and laments sang flat and sharp just beneath the unmelodic squawking.

The white-haired man behind the steering wheel of the fifteen-passenger van jolted as the car behind him rammed into his back bumper. He looked over his shoulder. "Where does the fool think I can go? Traffic is moving by inches. The military has checkpoints setup on every road into Colorado."

A man half the age of the driver stared out the back window. "Dad, he's frothing at the mouth. We have to get out of here."

The older man took in his surroundings. "We'll have to swim. We need to avoid the uniforms. Grab your knapsacks. Let's go."

The man, his wife, his two sons and their wives, five grandchildren, a family friend, and a German shepherd poured from the vehicle and slid down the embankment to the lazy river below. At this point, it was shallow, only chest high on the men.

Once across, the group made its way into thick foliage. They crept forward hoping to avoid the authorities.

A glow in the western sky caused them to pause and look back. "Move!" commanded the older man.

They picked up pace, hurtling through the trees. The man glanced back once more, his heart breaking at the loss of life and more. He considered the serpentine line of cars crawling eastward, ever eastward. For most of the occupants it would not be enough. Any sign of contamination would force them back the way they had come.

Peter Pryor turned his back, determined to survive, and followed his family.

Part One

Connections

1
My Father's World

A hot bath, a hearty meal, and a whole night's sleep helped Captain Laurel Moss put her current predicament into perspective. She stretched and yawned as a mellow sunshine bathed her through gauzy mauve curtains. A contented sigh involuntarily escaped her lips. She could not remember the last time she had slept an entire night without being disturbed by either war or nightmares. The curtains fluttered in the gentle breeze, and a mockingbird landed on the windowsill.

Laurel's dark-brown eyes fluttered open as the chirping sounded so much like an old hymn she had sung as a child when her grandmother took her to church. The young woman lifted herself to her elbows, her auburn hair hanging to her mid-back. The bight-eyed bird cocked its head at her and continued to sing merrily as if nothing bad existed in the world.

"Ugh," she grunted as she moved and felt the soreness in her muscles. "Well, pain still exists here," she muttered to herself. "This isn't Heaven." She felt the sutures in her shoulder. *Am I really on an island with dragons? Or was that just a dream? Did Stevens and I crash and somehow survive to be washed ashore here? Who stitched me up? Surely not that gorgeous boy.* "Boy," she said aloud. Realizing she wore only a sleeveless cotton shift, she bolted up straight. *Did he dress me? How did I get here? Where exactly am I?*

She staggered from the bed. On a chair in front of a dressing table with a mirror lay loose fitting pants and a shirt in soft brushed bronze cotton. She slipped them on and made her way down the stairs of the house. The smell of sausage frying lured her to the unknown.

Following her nose, she wandered into a kitchen that seemed as modern as any back home. A tall blond-haired young man flipped pancakes. He did not turn when she entered the room. "Did you sleep well, Captain Moss?"

"Yes, for the first time in ages." *The boy! How did he know I was here? I'm barefoot and didn't make a sound.*

The man plopped a stack of pancakes onto a plate and slid it and the sausage and syrup toward the end of the table where the woman stood. "Hungry?" he asked with a flawless smile.

"Starved." She sank into the chair and dug in without hesitation.

She thinks I'm cute. The young man grinned. "Well, at least you appreciate the native's culinary skills."

She choked down a bite as the man brought a glass of milk to her. "About that comment. Sorry. But you did come off a little strong calling me your sunrise."

"I suppose I did. It's just that you look like a sunrise, but maybe not mine. Can we start over?" He held out his hand. "Hi. I'm Aidan Alexander O'Rourke. Care to tell me how you washed up on my island like seaweed?"

Laurel laughed and shook his hand. "Captain Laurel Elaine Moss, United States Navy. It's a long story."

Aidan's eyes danced as he served himself a plate and sat in the chair adjacent to the one Laurel was using. "Going anywhere soon? Tell me your story."

"All right, if you tell me yours."

"Be glad to."

"First," said Laurel around a mouthful. "Where's Stevens? How is he? Where's my uniform?"

Aidan held up a hand. "It's all right. What's left of your uniform is being cleaned and mended. Lieutenant Stevens had to stay with Uncle Craig at the hospital."

"Hospital? Here?" the navy flier interrupted.

"It's small, but we have a hospital. It's on the big island. We put you in our home last night. We're on Isla Linda." The defensiveness in Aidan's voice was not wasted on Laurel. "Uncle Craig is a doctor. He came here from Pennsylvania," he continued. "You needed a few stitches, and Uncle Craig gave you a strong herbal sedative. Stevens's injuries required surgery, but he'll be fine."

"But you're like, um, primitive."

Aidan laughed. "I'll let you decide that, but I think we're quite progressive, and so does my dad."

"Where is he?"

"About his world doing whatever he does. He's Governor of Draconis, and he's attending to state affairs."

"State affairs?"

"Well, we did discover two United States Navy fliers on our shores. One of them said there's a war going on out there." His emerald eyes stretched wide. "Care to elaborate?" He dove into his breakfast.

Laurel swallowed. "I suppose I should." She drank the glass of milk without stopping for a breath. Aidan smirked.

"Okay," she began. "There has not been real peace since the 9/11 attacks before we were born. But about ten years ago, the North Koreans finally developed a guidance system that allowed them to launch a nuclear warhead at San Francisco. The first one fell into the ocean before it detonated, but it caused a tidal wave. Many northern Californians fled, knowing another attack would come because diplomacy was not working." She looked at her empty glass. "Got any coffee?"

"Sure." Aidan got up and poured coffee from an old-fashioned percolator attached to an electrical outlet.

Laurel pointed. "Electricity."

Aidan grinned. "Not so primitive?"

"Yeah." She started to say something else.

Aidan waved both hands and shook his head. "Uh-huh. My story later."

"Oh, all right." She scowled at being put off. "Well, the Koreans launched another which made much of the Pacific Northwest radioactive. Last reports were limited exposure possible, but only habitable by indestructible cockroaches." She shivered and grimaced. "I hate those things."

"Okay," Aidan prompted to keep her on track.

"You have no idea how big those things get in Miami." She rolled her eyes. "Needless to say, we retaliated from our Pacific bases. The Koreans formed alliances with China and several Middle Eastern countries. Then, one of them launched a biological weapon toward Israel, but it went off course and hit another Arab nation. After that, the

Koreans sent one of those bio-chem monsters toward Los Angeles. It made impact. Those exposed who didn't die have mutated."

"Mutated? To what?"

She nodded vigorously. "Yeah, they're still human, but they seem to have regressed back to Neanderthals. They're violent, and they can't abide direct sunlight. The few I've seen have like white eyes. There have been reports of actual foaming at the mouth like rabid dogs and cannibalism."

"So, where were you fighting?"

"Oh, that. Yeah, well, over a period of two years from the first attack almost every country became involved and was hit somehow. Midwest U.S., the East Coast, and the Gulf States, Western Europe, some of South America, far north Canada and Alaska, parts of Africa, Mexico, and Australia are relatively safe. Central Europe and Eastern Europe, especially the countries close to Asia and those Asian countries got hit hard." She got up and refilled her coffee cup.

Aidan heaved an exasperated sigh.

"Be patient," Laurel snapped. She sat back down. "This war has dragged on for ten years. Even Switzerland has activated forces to patrol its borders. There continue to be hit and run missions and threats of more nuclear or biological and chemical warfare. I've flown bombing raids over North Korea, China, the Persian Gulf region, and lots of other places. Stevens and I took off from an aircraft carrier near the tip of India. We flew into some pea-soup fog and none of our gauges would work. Then we were hit by what felt like a missile. The next thing I knew, you were calling me your sunrise." She grinned.

Aidan gave her a lopsided smirk. "I guess that was overreacting to your appearance. Tell me about where you grew up."

"Tough childhood. My grandmother raised me. Mom died of cancer. Dad died in Iraq. I lived in south Florida." She slapped her forehead. "Ooh! That's right. Your dad is Troy Tomerson, a.k.a. Rennin O'Rourke. Thought to be dead, but not! He was from Miami and played quarterback for the Raiders."

"Yeah. Laurel. Is it all right if I call you Laurel?"

"Yeah, sure. Just not Sunrise."

"What do you know about your grandfather or your other grandparents?"

"Dad was an orphan. My grandfather dropped off the face of the planet about the same time as your dad according to my grandmother."

"What was his name?"

"Lieutenant Colonel Clifton Spell. He was supposedly some badass Black Ops dude."

"Yeah." Aidan took the breakfast dishes to the sink.

"That was a weird sounding yeah." Laurel came to stand beside the young man. "Damn! Running water too. You got some explaining to do yourself, Mr. Island Native."

Aidan dropped the dish towel on the countertop. "I suppose I do. More than you know. Care for a tour?"

"I'd like that."

Walking toward the front door of the O'Rourke home, Laurel stopped abruptly and stared at a panorama of scenes from Draconian history painted on an entire granite wall of the large open family room. She pointed. "That wall is rock."

"Yeah." Aidan nodded. "The house is built onto a cave." He chuckled. "Does that make me a caveman?"

The young naval officer scowled. "I apologize again for sounding so callused."

"I'm not mad. I just thought it was funny. Do you want to see what's behind the granite wall?"

"Behind it? How?"

Aidan held up a long, thin index finger. "Watch and listen." Aidan walked to the wall and placed his palm flat against it. "*Tutus*."

The wall melted away. Laurel's jaw dropped. Aidan held out his hand. "Come on. It's safe—now."

Laurel followed him down steep stone steps. He reached the side of a long tunnel and flipped on several hanging lights. Rooms lined the tunnel walls. Aidan said, "Many years ago, a witch named Quazel created this underground fortress. It can only be entered through the use of magic. My sister, d'Aubigné, has given it a new phrase, '*Tutus*.' It means haven. Quazel kept my multiple-great-grandmother, Morgan Fitzpatrick, prisoner here for years. The Aidan O'Rourke who came five centuries ago to break the evil witch's curse on this land rescued her. Morgan married Aidan's son, Rennin, and they left Draconis and ended up in America. Years later, my father came back because the land needed another savior, and the dragons believed it had to be an O'Rourke. This place was being used to sacrifice virgins by another witch who had somehow managed to resurrect Quazel's spirit and had taken it into herself. D'Aubigné disintegrated her with a magical blast. Daddy built his house onto the cave to ensure it could never be used for evil again."

As they walked down the long hall, Aidan opened doors to show Laurel how the rooms were being used. One was a music room; another, Rennin O'Rourke's home office. When they arrived at the former sacrificial chamber, Aidan opened the door to a game room. "Nothing evil here now."

Laurel shook her head in disbelief. "No, it's quite homey. How many people know the magic phrase?"

"Anyone who can get inside our house is welcome to come down here."

They walked back toward the entrance. The wall had reappeared. Laurel touched it and said, "*Tutus.*" She inhaled sharply when nothing happened. She turned luminous bitter-chocolate eyes to the man. "Am I a prisoner?"

Aidan shook his head. "Nope." He touched the wall and said, "*Amach ar an saol.*"

The wall dissolved. Laurel looked up at the young man as they exited. "What does that one mean?"

"Out into the world." He opened the front door. "Shall we?"

She smiled and nodded.

Stepping out the door brought the couple to a pebbly incline leading to a pristine white beach lapped by aquamarine waves. Looking back, it was easy to see the house nestled against the rock face. The house front was irregular orange-yellow quartz set in mortar. Wooden stairs led to the beach.

The minute they walked onto the steps, Aidan called, "Moonbeam! I need a lift."

Laurel cocked her eyebrow in question. "Where's the dragon?"

"The main island. They have clefts as homes in the sheer rock face. I'll show you around. By the time we get to the meadow, she'll be here."

The first thing Laurel saw as they trekked along the shoreline was the reflection of sun on the rooftops of the houses built on Isla Linda. In awe she murmured, "You use solar energy?"

"Yes, and wind." Aidan pointed out several windmills camouflaged to resemble palm trees.

"Fascinating. You really are progressive rather than primitive."

The young man shrugged. "My dad is very scientific. So is Uncle Cliff."

"Uncle Cliff?"

"Um. Yeah."

Laurel narrowed her eyes. "All right, Mr. Caveman, who the hell is Cliff? Is there something I should know?"

"Well, yes. Daddy thought I might be able to tell you easier than grown-ups."

"Tell me what?" She balked, arms akimbo.

"Let's finish our tour. I'll explain as we fly to Draconis. Okay?"

The woman set her lips in a fine line of determination and took a deep steadying breath through her nose.

"Please?" Aidan said with wide green eyes. "I'd really like for you to see the meadow where Morgan and Rennin played. My dad has made it a park." He grabbed her hand and pulled her along more swiftly. "Nobody can build here." He swept his hand out to show the lush, verdant meadow with only a pavilion and old-fashioned porch-type swings scattered sparingly.

Laurel gasped at the sight. "Even Uncle Cliff?" she asked with a knot beginning to form in her stomach.

Aidan released a long sigh. "Uncle Cliff chose to have a small cottage in the mountains because it reminds him of the Himalayas where he was the happiest before he came here." He looked down at the ground then up. "Uncle Cliff is retired Lieutenant Colonel Clifton Spell."

"My grandfather!" Laurel's shriek could be heard on Draconis. Every dragon turned heads toward Isla Linda.

A silvery young female landed beside Aidan. "I think I timed my arrival perfectly." She set teeth together in what was intended to be a dragon's smile.

2

Long-Lost Relatives

In the meeting of Draconian officials on the big island in the large cavern called Alexander's Cavern, the humans took note of the dragons' reaction. Rennin O'Rourke raised an eyebrow while Cliff Spell sighed. "I take it he told her," said the grandfather.

"Yes," intoned Char, an inky black beast and Cliff's specially bonded dragon, in his sandpaper voice. "And she is more than a little bit upset."

"As expected," said Cliff.

"Yes," agreed Draco, the eldest of the dragons. His pearly white scales reflected the colors of the rainbow as he turned his head back toward the meeting of state heads. "But this could become ugly if Aidan responds as a child."

"My grandfather?" Laurel screamed again. "That bastard has been here all this time?"

"Whoa!" asserted Aidan. "Don't talk about Uncle Cliff like that."

"What should I do? Embrace my long-lost relative with open arms?"

"Well, yeah." Aidan's blond curls bobbed with enthusiasm.

"Why the hell would I do that? He left me!" She pointed around randomly, not sure which direction was right. "Out there! He left me to suffer!"

"No, he didn't."

"What do you know, Island Boy? Gram told me she sent him information. She almost died! They took me. They stuck me in a home for orphans until Gram was well enough to fight to get me back." She rubbed her arms as if she were cold. "And he was here in this utopia."

"It wasn't like that."

"Yeah?" She jabbed her finger into Aidan's chest with each question she asked. "How many monster-sized Florida cockroaches crawled on him in his sleep? How many dirty old men tried to put their hands where they didn't belong on him? How many nights did he go to bed hungry? How often did he cry until he fell asleep? How many times did he have nightmares about watching his flesh peel from his bones after an atomic bomb was dropped on him? How often did he curl into the fetal position and shake with uncontrollable fear? I want to see him. I want to see him right now!"

Aidan clutched her small hand firmly in one twice its size. "Not until you calm down. You don't know the whole story."

She jerked her hand away. "Let go of me! The whole story?" She tossed her head like an angry filly and stomped a foot as a horse pawing the ground. "That the happiest he ever was before now was in the Himalayas with his wife? That he never cared enough for my grandmother to stand beside her?"

"Stop!" Aidan pointed sharply at her. "Uncle Cliff didn't know a thing about your mother. Maybe your grandmother should have told him he had a daughter. That way he would have been in a position to take care of all of you. Get your facts straight, Solar Flare. Sunrises are beautiful!" He flipped his hands in the air in a gesture of giving up. "Not demented!"

"Ooh!" The next thing Aidan knew, Laurel came across with a right hook that made painful contact with his jaw. "That bastard took care of that other woman and the kid she had, or did he desert her too?"

Aidan rubbed his jaw. "You...will...never...hit...me...again," he said with measured deliberation.

From the corner of her eye, Laurel saw a wisp of smoke rising from the nostrils of the shiny silver dragon whose head pivoted back and forth from her to Aidan. Laurel snarled, "Or what? You'll get your dragon to eat me?"

"You'd give Moonbeam indigestion."

The dragon chuckled.

Laurel scowled. "Well, just what did my grandfather do with his other family?"

"His wife died, murdered. Your aunt Ming is here. She's married to Jacques and they have a family. *You* have a family."

"Right. I'm so sure they want me."

Seeming to lose energy, she sank to the downy grass shoots. Aidan sat beside her. "They do. When Uncle Cliff found out about you, he tried to go back to Florida, but he couldn't get past the barrier. He tried repeatedly over the years, even as recently as last month."

Tears dripped down Laurel's cheeks, and she pulled blades of grass as she looked at the ground. Aidan lifted her chin. "It's true." He chuckled softly. "But don't ever hit Ming like you did me. She'll kick your ass from sunrise to sunset."

Barely above a whisper, Laurel said, "I've never had anyone but my grandmother. Now, I'm here, and I don't know how to help her. Did Cliff really try to come to us?"

A soft grunt escaped the young man's lips. "You'll find I'm honest to a fault. I don't lie well."

"Uh-hum," vibrated a throaty summons from the dragon. "My own grandfather carried him to the barrier more than once."

"You have a grandfather?" Laurel's curiosity piqued.

Moonbeam bobbed her head. "Smoke is my father, and Char, Cliff's bonded dragon, is my grandfather."

"Bonded dragon?"

"Yes. Some humans form special bonds with certain dragons. I am Aidan's bonded dragon."

Laurel stood and touched Moonbeam's nose. "You think I could have one?"

"Time will tell. Do you still want to see your grandfather?"

Laurel looked back at Aidan. "I've calmed down."

"So, it seems." He spread his hand, open palm up, toward Moonbeam. "Climb aboard my low-maintenance aircraft."

"Hm." Laurel closed her eyes and shook her head. "I must have sounded like a real bitch."

Aidan rubbed his jaw again. "Well, let's just say you're feisty. You pack a wallop."

The two of them mounted the magnificent form of transport, and Moonbeam lifted into the air.

Draco looked toward Cliff. "Well, she might explode again, but she's on her way here. Are you ready to meet your granddaughter?"

"Absolutely."

Rennin slapped his hand on top of the marble table. "Then let's adjourn for now. Let's meet back after lunch to discuss what, if any, involvement we might have in the outside situation."

The mayors and other representatives from each township, the dragon council with the exception of Char, and Rennin O'Rourke with his select cabinet returned to their own homes until the afternoon. Astride Smoke's back, Rennin waved to Aidan and Laurel as the father and daughter dragons passed each other in the conveyance of their bonded humans.

Sitting behind the woman with one hand resting on either of her thighs, Aidan spoke into her ear. "I've been thinking about the things you said when you were ranting about your grandfather."

"So what?"

"Maybe I'm being too forward again, but you said something about a dirty old man. Still, the first thing, which must bother you more, was cockroaches."

Laurel shivered. "I hate those things."

"More than dirty old men?"

"Yes. The dirty old man got hit upside the head with a frying pan by his wife when I screamed my head off. She had him arrested. Those roaches are indestructible. One of them bit me once. I don't care if experts say they don't bite. They even survived the nuclear fallout. I bet they might have bitten people who mutated."

"What does a cockroach look like? I don't think I've ever seen one."

She craned her neck to look behind her, thinking Aidan was joking. His face was serious. "Really? There aren't any on Draconis?"

"I don't know."

Laurel described with gross exaggeration the appearance and size of cockroaches.

"Seriously, ten inches, Laurel? I've seen dragonflies with ten-inch wing spans, but it sounds as if a roach is some kind of beetle."

"Beetles on steroids. Shells so hard they crunch if you do manage to step on one. And the flying ones dive-bomb you. And they *never* come alone. If you see one, *thousands* more are hiding, just waiting. I swear to

God, they seek revenge if you kill one. I can just see an army lined up with a commander roach clicking out orders." She shivered from head to toe.

"You're scared of an insect, but not spiders?"

"No! Spiders are beneficial to the ecosystem. Besides, they can eat detestable cockroaches."

Aidan laughed. "You really are scared to death of a bug."

"Not just any bug—cockroaches."

"I thought the word *fear* didn't exist in your vocabulary."

She cringed. "Well. That's a phobia. I'm not afraid of anything else."

"If you say so."

They set down own a landing outside a mammoth cave opening. Laurel shivered. "It's cold here."

"Sorry. I should've made sure you had a jacket." He glanced down. "And shoes. There's even snow up here. We ski."

The odd trio ambled down a corridor, finally arriving at the large chamber in Alexander's Cavern. Only two beings awaited them. The massive black dragon and the smaller silver dragon exchanged what could only be described as dragon hugs, touching alternately cheek to cheek on both sides, much like Europeans greeted one another with a kiss to both cheeks.

Staring at the tall, lean, tanned man with jet black hair streaked with silver and fathomless, nearly black eyes, Laurel barely heard Char introduce himself before he excused himself, his granddaughter, and Aidan. Char nudged Aidan with his nose to leave Cliff and Laurel alone. The older, wiser dragon prodded his granddaughter and her bonded human to the outside landing. Char whispered to the two, "We'll wait here. If she hits him, I'll scare her." He gave a dragon grin and winked one golden eye. The two dragons settled onto the ledge, and Aidan reclined against Moonbeam.

Laurel still stared at Cliff Spell. He stared back, taking in every angle of the young woman he had never been able to hug. He finally broke the silence. "You look so much like Margaret. Except your eyes. I think you have my eyes."

Blinking hard to keep tears in check, Laurel said, "Aidan said you tried to come for me. I wish you had."

"I'm so sorry. Draco tried to visit your dreams and kept me informed that you were all right even if you struggled."

The former military Special Forces officer retrieved a piece of paper. His hand shook as he handed it to the girl. "I read this after I got here. If I had taken time to open it before we set sail, I could have brought both of you with me."

The words of the letter burned into the young naval officer's heart as she read. She looked up at the man she had always wanted to know. "You really never knew about my mother."

"No, I didn't. My wife, Mai Tai, was murdered. When I met Margaret, I was still mourning. I cared a great deal for your grandmother, but at that time I wasn't ready to let myself fall in love." He took the letter back, folding and replacing it in its envelope. "Still, I would've been a father to my child. I would probably even have married Margaret. I have a deep sense of honor."

The auburn-haired girl twisted her hands together. "Just so you know, Draco succeeded in coming to me on several occasions. I used to pretend I was on an island with dragons. My friends thought I was crazy, so I stopped saying anything and just went along."

Cliff shuffled his feet. "You wanna sit?"

"No." She shook her head. "I'd like the kind of greeting Moonbeam got from *her* grandfather."

Cliff took a few steps forward and performed the routine Char had done with Moonbeam. "Like that?"

Nervous giggles bubbled from Laurel. "Not quite."

The man pulled the young woman into an embrace. "Oh, little one, how I have longed to do this."

Laurel slipped her arms around her grandfather's waist, moving her hands up to lock onto his shoulders. "Grandpa." She let her face rest in the comfort of his hard, muscular chest, feeling the gentle pulsating of his heart.

After a time, Cliff led his granddaughter to a comfortable over-stuffed love seat. "Tell me about your grandmother. Is she well?"

Laurel nodded. "She's been cancer free for a long time now." She looked her grandfather in the eyes. "Will you bring her here now?"

He nodded. "Yes, if I can."

"You have a daughter here, and other grandchildren?"

"I do, indeed."

"When can I meet them?"

"Now, if you'd like.

With her hand nestled in the crook of his arm, grandfather and granddaughter walked onto the ledge where Aidan, Char, and Moonbeam waited. Aidan sprang to his feet as the two dragons eyed the duo.

"Everything's fine," assured Cliff. "We're going to meet Ming and family."

"Need company, Uncle Cliff?" asked Aidan.

The older man shook his head. "Not right now. Char, will you give us a lift?"

"Naturally," the black dragon's voice rasped.

Aidan gazed at the young woman. "Will you be staying with your grandfather, or will you need a ride?"

Laurel looked into matching eyes. "I think I'll stay with Grandpa. Thanks, Island Boy."

"My pleasure, Sun..." The expression on the girl's face stopped Aidan short. "My pleasure, Captain. Glad the native could be of service."

Aidan climbed onto Moonbeam and chuckled against the dragon's neck. "Home. She likes me."

"Oh, yes, I can tell," agreed the beast. "Oil and water—fire and ice—a fine combo."

Char laughed softly as he overheard the exchange. "Well, come on. I think Ming might be expecting you."

Char winged his way to the heart of Draconis and set down in a cleared area near homes bustling with activity. As Cliff and Laurel walked toward one of the houses, he pointed out others. "Tyler and d'Aubigné Bishop live there." He nodded. "Dr. Craig and Casey Jamison, Bobby and Jennifer Willis, and Harvey and Nicole Zane. They all have children your age and a little older or younger." He stopped in

33

front of the house that had belonged the Diggory and Elizabeth Danaher. "This is where Jacques and Ming Picard live. They have three children: C.D., Mai Tzu, and Jackie. Mai Tzu is the only girl."

Cliff lifted his hand and knocked resoundingly on the back door of the house. A petite Asian woman, who did not look a day over twenty, but was in her early forties, open. "Papa!" Ming hugged her father. She turned to Laurel with a radiant smile on her face. She held her arms open. Laurel felt pulled to her aunt's embrace. Ming kissed her niece's cheek. "We have much to catch up on. I pray we have the time, but I feel an urgency to deal with the disturbance outside. Come in. Let's talk."

3
A Difference of Opinion

The expression on Jacques Picard's face did not reflect his wife's. "What's going on?" Cliff demanded as the tension was palpable.

Ming waved a hand in dismissal. "We're having a difference of opinion."

Laurel watched in strange amazement as Jacques seemed to be the one performing the household tasks. The man bustled about preparing the noon meal. Cliff closed his eyes and inhaled the aroma. "Jamaican jerk chicken salad. How did you know I was coming?"

Jacques mumbled, "A leetle birdy told us."

"Green or red?" asked Cliff.

"Green," Jacques replied. "Esmeralda told me to expect zhou." He finally smiled toward Laurel. "And my niece." He planted a kiss on her cheek. "Yes, to zhour unasked question. We are argueeng about eenvolvement een zee war outside."

"Oh," sighed Laurel. "My presence has caused a great deal of trouble."

"Not your fault," assured Ming. "Sit down."

The two newcomers found chairs around an oblong dining table. Ming called out the door in a voice loud enough to carry for miles. Laurel wondered how someone so small could belt the summons to lunch at that volume. Three adolescents appeared in short order. The eldest appeared to be just younger than Laurel, the second was a budding teen, and the youngest looked about ten. Cliff introduced the lot.

Within a quarter hour, Jacques placed the food on the table, and after a quick blessing of the meal, organized chaos ensued. The dishes passed around the table in order, and each person served his or her own plate. Laurel hesitated only slightly when the first bowl reached her. Then, because she so rarely had such appetizing and hearty food, she followed her grandfather's example and helped herself, devouring every bite even after the huge breakfast Aidan had prepared for her.

After the meal, the youngsters saw to cleanup while the hosts and guests moved to the living room. Shortly, the back door slammed as the three children left the house. Still feeling a bit uncomfortable, Laurel observed, "I saw some pretty cool things about Draconis, but isn't there a school?"

Jacques laughed. "Yes, zere ees school. Zis happens to be zee weekend."

"Oh." Laurel's face burned from the blood flooding it. "I seem to have lost track of time."

"It's okay," said Ming. "Weekends generally have lots of family activity, but the arrival of new family has made for State activity."

"Sorry," said Laurel. She tried to point to a direction again without success. "I give up. Anyway, my world is in turmoil. I have to go back. I won't ask any of you to go, but I need to know how to get back. How has this caused great State activity?"

"Some of us want to go and fight with you," said Ming.

"Some of us," said Jacques with is big brown eyes stretched as wide as they would go, "love zee peace here. We are afraid of loseeng zat."

"I see," said Laurel. "I take it, Ming, that you want to go."

"Yes."

"Not you?" Laurel looked to Jacques.

"I hate fighteeng. Eef we Meeng and I both go, who weell care for zee sheeldren? In a leetle while, weell meet with Reeneen and zee heads of state to deescuss what to do."

"Of course, he's the governor. What do you think he'll say?" She looked to her grandfather.

Cliff shrugged. "I'm military. I say join the fight. Rennin will be hesitant. Most likely he'll tell us to follow our consciences. But the dragons...I don't know. Char will not want to fight, but he'll go with me. Smoke is Rennin's bonded dragon, but he has a temper and will want to defend anyone we love. Brindle will go wherever Craig goes. Draco will most likely mediate and designate troops to go if that is the decision. He probably will not venture into that world. Only Char and Smoke have ever gone there. But dragon fire is as powerful as any atomic weapon without the lasting devastation. And they move as fast as most planes, if not faster."

Laurel popped a hand over her mouth and mumbled between her fingers. "Oh, my God! I never dreamed of asking the dragons to fight." Her eyes lit up. "A secret weapon that could end this war."

"At what cost?" asked Jacques.

An hour later, Laurel walked into the the grand chamber she had been in earlier. This time a good number of humans and seven dragons were present. She felt as if all eyes were upon her. She slipped her hand into her grandfather's for the safety it afforded her.

The human representatives from every area of Draconis sat around a massive shiny oval marble table. The dragons contented themselves to perch on the overhanging ledge above the chamber. Laurel recognized Smoke from the beach, Char from the morning, and Draco from her dreams. In addition to the three she recognized, there were a brilliant scarlet dragon, a bit smaller than Char and Draco but a little larger than Smoke; a sparkling floresent green dragon about the size of the red; a huge mohagany with flecks of beige and tawny; and a smaller soft beige one that kept close to the mahogany one. Laurel whispered, "Where's Moonbeam? Where's Aidan?"

Cliff whispered back to her, "Both too young to be in government yet."

Rennin O'Rourke occupied the chair at the far end of the oval table away from the entrance. With the exception of Rennin having dark hair and Aidan being blond, they could have been carbon copies. A man with feiry red hair sat to his left. The chair to his right was vacant as was the one beside it. The chairs directly beside the carrot top were also empty with a shorter, stockier bald man just beside them. Jacques and Ming took those seats, and Cliff steered Laurel to the vacant chair not directly to Rennin's right. He took the seat next to Rennin.

Rennin looked around. "Is everyone here?"

Under her breath Laurel said, "I wish Aidan was here."

Rennin gave a nod to Smoke who rumbled from the cave. Within minutes, the smokey-gray dragon returned with Moonbeam and Aidan.

A bit of snorting could be heard behind the creatures, and a wisp of smoke curled to their backsides.

Aidan slid down Moonbeam's wing to the chamber while the young silvery beast settled next to her father. The creature's eyes darted around the room, and she flicked a look over her shoulder.

Aidan brought a chair from somewhere in the depths of the recesses and planted himself beside his father. Rennin placed a hand on the boy's shoulder. "Now, is everyone here?" Rennin asked again, a slight smirk playing around his mouth. Aidan whispered to his father. "Really?" Rennin asked.

Then he turned his gaze upward. "Draco, it seems your son is a bit angry he has not been invited to this meeting. Considering his betrothed is here and the gravity of the situation, perhaps it's time he joined in the decision-making."

The teeth together in a dragon smile unnerved Laurel each time she saw it. Draco delivered the grin. "When he stops behaving like an impetuous child, I'll ask him to enter. Moonbeam is acting quite decorus."

Down a corridor that could not be seen from the meeting chamber floor a voice wailed, "Father, please?"

Draco wagged his head. "Hundreds of years waiting for an egg and I get the most impatient creature ever hatched."

Moonbeam nudged the older dragon with her nose and batted stick-like dragon lashes at him. "Please?" she asked quietly.

"Very well." The lustrous white beast granted permission. "Filigree, come on, but sit with Moonbeam and just listen unless asked directly for a response."

A young dragon so golden that light reflecting off his scales could blind a human darted in and nestled down beside his intended mate. "Not a word, I promise."

Draco lifted a talon and touched his mouth. Filigree snapped his jaws tight. Draco turned to Rennin. "Everyone is here."

"Then we need to get down to business. Order." Rennin addressed Laurel. "Captain Moss, will you please tell everyone present what is going on in the world beyond Draconian waters?"

She stood. "Oh, yes."

Rennin held up a hand. "Everyone, this is Captain Laurel Elaine Moss of the United States Navy. She's a flier of an aircraft and also Clifton Spell's granddaughter. As you know, for years the barrier has been sealed, and Cliff could not return to the outside world to bring Laurel and his other family here. Somehow, she has been brought to us. Make her welcome after the meeting. Now, Captain, please tell us the story."

Laurel related her story once again, making eye contact with Aidan often. Somehow his presence either made her angry or calmed her frenzied thoughts. She concentrated hard on the facts of the war and tried to shake the butterflies in her stomach as she looked at the young man who could have been a Norse god.

When she finished, she sat back beside her grandfather. Rennin again addressed the gathering. "After such a long sealing of the barrier, Captain Moss's presence is significant. It seems the war out there has become our war, but on what level? Some of you have already voiced the need to go and fight." He looked directly at Cliff and Ming. "I'm not convinced this is Draconis's war."

Laurel blurted, "But if you help, we can end this war."

"And to the victor go the spoils," Rennin said with his eyebrow arched, his emerald eyes that looked just like his son's flashing anger. "What would Draconis get for entering a war with no defined enemy and no known ally?"

The dragons fidgeted with energy. Laurel pointed. "They could end this tomorrow."

Rennin sighed. "Do you really think the world out there is ready for dragons? When they were in that realm centuries ago, mankind tried to destroy them. Why risk that again? Why risk the peace enjoyed here?"

Cliff cleared his throat. "I will not in good conscience ask you or any other citizen of Draconis to go to war, but I have to go back if only to find Margaret and bring her here. There are others who may still be alive, Rennin. Peter Pryor? What about Jake Muñoz's family? The man died in your stead. Laurel has said some escaped the West Coast disaster. Don't you feel you owe them something? At least a rescue attempt?"

"And who would you expect to accompany you, Cliff?"

"I'll go with my grandfather," said Laurel.

"As you should," said Rennin, "but you're not a citizen of Draconis."

"I'll go with my father," Ming asserted.

Jacques huffed. "Zhou have a fameely, sheeldren."

"This kind of war knows no boundaries, no age limit," argued Ming. "It knows no gender, and"—She caught the eye of Scarlet, Char's mate and Ming's bonded dragon—"it honors no species. How many canines and dolphins have died in war? What about war horses through the ages? Rennin, you cannot dictate actions this time. You need to let conscience be the guide."

A low rumble sounded above. Char's rasping voice said, "If Cliff fights, I fight with him."

"Father!" Smoke could not believe what he had heard. Char loved peace.

The next voice that surprised all present was Scarlet. "And I will go with my husband and Ming."

"No!" Smoke opposed his parents openly.

The ledge shook as Draco stood. Small pebbles fell to the floor below. "Nothing will be accomplished with this difference of opinion," the pearly white dragon intoned. "This war outside will not cause civil war on this island. This is a time to pray and consider all. With your leave, Governor, let us meet again tomorrow. If we are to join the battle, much must be put in place."

"Well said, Draco," Rennin said. "We will reconvene tomorrow at one. Adjourned."

Those in attendance began to exit. Rennin walked to stand beneath the ledge where Draco stood. "What are you planning, wise one?"

"I must exercise my special ability. I will need d'Aubigné."

4
A Distant View

Laurel left her grandfather's side to get to Aidan. "Who's the ruler of Draconis?"

The girl's sarcasm was not lost on the heir to the governorship. "Smartass. Draco and Daddy are a team. Draco knows humans would not follow a beast, so the dragons have determined an O'Rourke must always be governor."

"So? You're next in line?"

"Yes."

"Wow!" She sniggered. "And I thought you were just a native, not king."

"No kingship. No one person can pass a law. It must be voted upon."

The frown on Laurel's face etched her brow in lines. "I was trying to kid around."

"Sorry, but the idea of being governor someday is serious to me. And now with a possible war"—Aidan shrugged—"I'm concerned."

"How old are you again?"

"Seventeen."

"You seem a lot older."

"Old enough for your ancient nineteen years to enjoy a picnic with?"

Laurel rubbed her stomach. "I have eaten more in this one day than in the last six months."

Aidan dipped a corner of his mouth as he arched the corresponding eyebrow. The young woman held up her hand. "Exaggeration."

"So?"

"I'd like to see Stevens if possible. Then, sure. Why not?"

"Are you and Stevens a couple?"

"No." She glowered toward her would-be beau. "Subordinate officer. No way."

"Do you have a fellow?"

"I've been too busy fighting a war."

"Okay. Let's get you to your friend." He called after the red-haired man. "Uncle Craig!"

Dr. Craig Jamison stopped. "Yes?"

"Come on." Aidan motioned with his hand for Laurel to follow him. "Laurel, this is Dr. Jamison. He gave you those few stitches."

"Thanks." She held out her hand. Craig shook it. "How's Stevens? I'd like to see him," she said with a measure of authority.

"He's doing well. He's awake and has asked after you. I haven't told him about the dragons yet. Maybe you should."

"You have a good point, Dr. Jamison."

"You and Aidan come with me. Brindle will take us home." Craig signaled the flecked mahogany dragon.

"Your bonded?" Laurel pointed.

"Yes."

"He's massive."

"Brindle is large, but he has a sweet disposition, unlike me. I get riled easily. Your copilot is in a lot of pain. Don't upset him." Brindle set the humans on his back with tender care. "Tell him about our special friends with as much subtly as you can."

Laurel walked down the center wing of the three-wing, thirty-bed medical facility with Aidan at her side. Each wing had ten rooms, five on each side of the hallway. The main admissions and half a dozen exam rooms, including one surgical suite were at the front with the three short halls shooting off like sunrays off a child's drawing of the sun. Very little had been said on the trip from Alexander's Cavern. She broke the silence. "What are your thoughts on the war?"

"Are you asking if I plan to fight by your side?" He grinned down at her.

She blushed deep crimson. Aidan chuckled. "This is Stevens's room. I'll let you visit."

"His first name's Dale."

Aidan gave a slight nod and opened the door. He left Laurel to check on her navigator.

Lieutenant Dale Stevens cracked his eyes as the door made a soft sound. "Captain?" He tried to rise but sank back with a groan. "I thought you might be dead. I had the weirdest dream. There were dragons and one held me in its talons. These folks must have some good drugs. Where are we?"

Laurel pulled a chair from against the wall to the man's bedside. "This place is called Draconis. I'm glad you're lying down." She took his hand. "The dragons are real. This place exists in some parallel time or something."

"Are you shitting me?"

"Have I ever lied to you?"

"No. Not even when you told me my wife died."

"I won't start now."

"Okay. Am I done for?"

She patted his hand. "No. This place is very progressive. They use solar and wind power. The air is clean. This is their small hospital. The doctor actually trained in the States. The governor is none other than Troy Tomerson, quarterback for the Raiders. He supposedly died, but he's really Rennin O'Rourke. He was worth a fortune and just vanished."

"Before my time." The man began to drift off. "What kind of pain meds do they use?"

"All-natural herbs from what I've gathered."

"Cool. Let me rest, okay?"

She stood. "Yeah. We'll be here a little while. They're deciding whether or not to join the fight, and you have to heal. They'll get us back no matter."

"What if I don't want to go back?"

Laurel sighed. "Then I guess you died when our plane went down."

"You'd do that, wouldn't you?"

"You know I would."

Stevens yawned. "Yeah. I'm not gonna run, but will this war ever be over?"

"It will if the dragons help."

"Whatever you say, Captain…" He dropped to sleep.

When Laurel left the room, she heard female laughter near the entrance. She came into the lobby to find three young women, twin blondes and a redhead, who must serve as nurses gathered around Aidan. She felt a sudden unexplainable flare of anger as she stood at a distance and took in the view.

Aidan made eye contact from a distance and fought back his grin. *She's jealous. I won't tell her Caitlin and Morgan are my sisters and that Michelle Zane is almost like a sister until later, much later, when I have to. Let her smolder.*

A tall, lithe woman slid from the wing of the golden dragon, Filigree. Her chestnut hair hung in a braid to her lower back while her jade eyes danced with life. The silk emerald tunic she wore over loose silk slacks fluttered in the breeze.

Draco turned as the woman entered the meeting chamber. It appeared his golden eyes had a flame in them as he met the woman with his wings outspread. D'Aubigné O'Rourke Bishop leaned into the chest of the massive beast in an embrace of true affection. "Draco, how have you been? We haven't seen enough of each other lately."

"I'm well. You're more beautiful with each passing day."

"What do you need from me, wise one? You didn't summon me to flatter me."

"No. I need to exercise my ability to see beyond. You know I need your magic to see more than shadows of anything or anyone who is not bonded to one of my kind. I must see what's happening so we can decide what to do."

Rennin O'Rourke entered the chamber with a glass of wine for his eldest daughter. "Hello, my darling." They hugged and held onto each other for a long moment.

She took the glass and sipped. "Daddy, are you going to war?"

"It depends on what Draco sees. We'll vote after his quest."

"Draco, will you fight?" D'Aubigné seemed shocked that the white dragon would inflict harm on anyone.

"I have not fought since Quazel. I think I would rather lend my aid in other ways, but I cannot know until I look into that world."

"I understand. What do you need me to do? We haven't tried this for a long time. When the barrier was sealed, we could not see anything but shadows, no matter if there were connections to bonded humans."

"Yes, and even those shadows were disturbing."

"Shall we go to the precipice?"

"Yes, that's the clearest place." He held out an enormous talon. D'Aubigné grasped it and the dragon placed her on his back.

Rennin reached up to touch his daughter's leg. "We'll be back soon, Daddy," she said.

Draco took flight as soon as he reached the outside ledge. D'Aubigné gently stroked the glistening scales. "You're nervous."

"I'm frightened of what I'll see."

Landing on the highest point of the island, brought the duo to a snow-covered mountain peak. Draco blew fire into a pit so that his bonded human would not freeze. He looked out over the island. Behind him lay sheer cliffs filled with caves in which the dragons made homes. Ocean waves crashed ferociously against gigantic rocks at the bottom. In the near distance, loomed Isla Linda. Its granite quarries gleamed on one side as the other sported lush woodlands and grasslands. To his right was the settlement of Prairieville, its fields laden with grains. A strip of quasi-jungle leading to a narrow piece of desert and then the oasis where the town of King Satin's Realm existed appeared on his left. Below after a mountain range gleamed the pristine white beach where Laurel had washed ashore. The town bordering the beach was called Waterford. The sparse housing in the mountains themselves was designated Sierra Bluff.

Draco sighed. "Draconis has so much beauty. What if this war decimates my home as Quazel did so long ago?"

"We won't let that happen." D'Aubigné caressed the top of the dragon's head. "Let's do this."

The powerful young mage leaned against Draco's neck and placed her hands on each side of his head, just behind his eyes where the flesh was softer. Draco inhaled deeply and stared into the unknown.

Humans of all races screamed and scurried trying to avoid the fire. But there was no escape. Their skin melted and they were no more. Others moaned in agony. They were sick to the point of foaming at the mouth. Some tore into the flesh of weaker ones, devouring them as food. Still others huddled, although sick, together in unity. One worked tirelessly with formulas. Some seemed better. The cacophony of voices in all languages swirled around as if in a tornadic force. Dead, dying, decaying. And then—a bright light. Not another bomb. *Hope.*

Draco shook himself. "D'Aubigné, did you see it?"

"Yes. We have no choice."

"You will not go."

"No, not yet. I must stay behind. But Draconis will no longer be legend."

"It is time." Draco's voice was little more than a whisper.

5
I Feel It in My Bones

Draco and d'Aubigné returned to Alexander's Cavern where Rennin had waited. Anxious lines on the governor's face met his friend and daughter. "Well?" he asked, a knot in his stomach.

Before he spoke, Draco placed d'Aubigné on the ground. The pearly dragon intoned, "We're destined to join the fight. Draconis has reached the point to become one with that world."

"Oh," Rennin groaned and sank to the ground. "I felt it in my bones. What is your suggestion?"

"Daddy," d'Aubigné responded. "Put it to the vote. Deter none who wish to go."

"Even your brother?"

D'Aubigné leaned against Draco and closed her eyes. She knew how important her baby brother was to the future of Draconis. She sighed.

"Especially Aidan, Daddy. You have to let him be a man."

Rennin nodded. He stood, kissed his daughter, patted Draco, and called, "Smoke, I need you."

Barely a minute passed before Smoke joined the others. Rennin climbed onto his bonded dragon's back and the two flew to Isla Linda. The magnificent beast knew not to disturb the man's thoughts when he was so deeply contemplative.

Renée Peyton O'Rourke met her husband, her luminous blue eyes filled with worry. "What did Draco see?"

"I didn't get the details," Rennin answered. "But he said the time for one world has come. We're going to war, baby. I'm scared."

She held her arms open, and he fell into her embrace. "Don't fret, Rennin. We'll survive this. Will you be going?"

He scowled; Renée released a heavy sigh. "Dumb question. Aidan?"

"I don't know. We'll meet tomorrow. Draco will give his report, and then we'll make decisions."

"So, you're saying everyone has to follow his own conscience?"

"Yes. I won't give orders either way."

She walked away a few steps, her hand covering her mouth. "I'm staying here."

"Of course, you are. You and Craig will be needed here for medical purposes. D'Aubigné will stay here for this is where her magic is strongest, although there might be a time she'll need to venture out. Caitlin and Morgan will have to decide."

Renée shook her head. "The girls won't go, but Marshall and Randall might."

"They are their father's sons. I'll wager Zane will go, especially if I do."

"Are Ming and Jacques fighting about this? Aidan thought so."

"A little."

"Damn it!" She punched the air. "This war is already causing trouble here."

"I know, but let's find a silver lining—Aidan thinks he's found his sunrise." Rennin smirked, and his green eyes glistened with boyish mischief.

"Laurel?" Renée sniggered.

Rennin nodded.

Aidan's mother rolled her eyes. "Well, shit! Maybe—If she doesn't end up being his sunset. That redhead is a red flag waving."

"Let him make his own decisions, Renée."

She lifted her hands in surrender. "Far be it from Momma to have influence." She headed toward the kitchen.

Rennin caught her hand. "But you do. You hold sway over my every thought." He pulled her close and kissed her. "You are still heart of my heart, life of my life, and I will love you until the day I die."

"Let's hope it's not in the damned war."

He entangled his fingers in her short blonde hair. "Take me away, Renée, if only for a short time."

An hour later, the O'Rourke family still occupying the home on Isla Linda sat down to dinner. Aidan stuffed half a dozen taco shells to overflowing with ground beef, cheese, sour cream, lettuce, tomato, onion, and hot sauce. Staring at his plate, he crunched into the savory food.

Mother and father glanced at each other, concern over their son's silence evident from both expressions.

By the time Aidan had finished his third taco without uttering a word, Rennin cleared his throat. "Talk, son. Now."

Without looking up, Aidan mumbled, "Are we going to war?"

Rennin pushed back. "Tomorrow we'll hear Draco's report. Then, we'll decide."

"Daddy, I don't think we have a choice." He raised his eyes without his head lifting. "I mean, if Laurel and Stevens got through the barrier, others can. And they could be the enemy."

"Right now, we don't know who the enemy is."

Aidan's head popped up. "You don't think Laurel..."

"Stop," Rennin snapped. "Not her personally, but I honestly don't know about *any* government that actually uses nuclear, chemical, or biological weapons."

"But you're an American," Aidan argued.

"I was. Now I'm Draconian."

"But..."

"No." Rennin pointed a firm finger toward his son. "Even if I were still in the States, I would not approve any weapon that annihilates all living things."

"Dragons could annihilate lots."

Rennin frowned, furrowing his eyebrows in deep disgust. "I'd hope they would use their abilities to end the war, not life. I would never put that on them. Would you?"

Aidan thought about Moonbeam and her sweet disposition. He pictured Draco and could not imagine that dragon killing a single human. Smoke, on the other hand, might take out a continent if those he loved were threatened—but only if his loved ones were in mortal danger.

"No, sir," Aidan said through a long sigh. "But maybe they could help another way."

"That will be their decision. Let's finish dinner."

The time for the State meeting arrived in a blur of conversations. Never had Rennin had so much trouble gaining control.

Finally, with quiet, Rennin called the meeting to order. "As all of you know, yesterday, Draco exercised his special gift and looked into the future. He has never been able to see a definite outcome, only possibilities. I'll let him share what he saw."

Rennin looked to the ledge where the ancient being sat. "Draco."

With his wings spread, the massive dragon rose. "Thank you, Rennin. The last time I looked into the future, it was to find our leader. I tried a small glance to assure the well-being of Cliff's granddaughter. Yesterday's attempt was the most gut-wrenching experience. I saw indescribable misery for mankind and ultimate destruction of our home if we do nothing. I also saw a flash of hope that only we can give. We have no choice—we must offer our assistance. I know, though, that not all of us can or should go. A select few will be able to accomplish more. You must decide your place." Draco sat.

Rennin stood again and looked every representative in the eye. "We still have to vote. All in favor of offering assistance in ending the war beyond, a show of hands."

Only a couple of humans did not vote yea. The only dragon that did not vote affirmatively was Brindle.

"Brindle?" Rennin said, shocked the quiet dragon would not vote in favor of Draco's recommendation.

"I abstain. My heart will not allow me to vote for war, but I will offer what assistance I can in support of the Council's decision."

Draco said in backing of his friend, "Brindle, I do not ask for fighting, unless it is the only way. I feel it deep in my bones that we are not meant to fight, but to offer another solution."

"And I will support assistance." Brindle dipped his enormous head with half-closed eyes.

Rennin nodded. "Then, it is decided. Now, we must decide what kind of aid we have to offer."

He looked around the assembly, catching his son's eye.

"And to whom."

6
With or Without You

Rennin once again addressed Draco. "Wise one, did you discern a specific enemy?"

"I was able to ascertain the original aggressor, a people from a land in the far eastern part of the world. Since then, any true villain is hard to determine. Frequently, nations are imprisoning and killing their own. Many horrible things have resulted from the chemical and biological weapons used. The nuclear weapons destroy all life, but the other things kill some and change many more."

"Change? Can you explain?" Rennin asked.

The dragon shook his head. "Perhaps Captain Moss can give a better explanation. She has seen these animals, creatures, firsthand."

With a nod, Rennin turned his attention to the Navy flier. "Captain Moss?"

Laurel scrunched up her face. "Well, they aren't zombies because they aren't the walking dead. They do appear animalistic, even cannibalistic. The few I've seen have white eyes, kind of like completely covered with cataracts. They appear pale, and blister in direct sunlight. Even dark-skinned people have pallor, kind of washed out."

She bit her index finger knuckle in thought. "I saw two that had been captured. I never heard them speak, only grunt."

Craig spoke up. "Is the medical field doing anything to find something to reverse or at least arrest the effects?"

"I don't know," Laurel replied.

Harvey Zane gave a snort. "Craig, governments would rather eradicate the problems they caused."

"All right." Rennin held up a hand. "The first thing we must do is determine how we can be of help."

Laurel blurted, "The dragons could eliminate all threats."

Rennin glared at the girl. "Your own government included?"

"What?"

"Captain Moss," he went on, "I believe we will not back any government. We'll try to offer help of restoration. Dragons are not weapons. They are intelligent beings who feel the plight of mankind, yea of all mortal beings, deeply. Neither you nor I can ask them to kill."

Laurel looked toward Draco, who gave her a half smile. Though she knew it was a smile, seeing those enormous teeth still unnerved her. "I understand," she said. "So, exactly what is your plan, Mr. O'Rourke?"

"Recon. Then, when we gather intel, we can decide."

"I have to go back," Laurel said. "It's my duty. Stevens will also go back."

"I understand that," said Rennin. "I think both of you need a little healing time. When Dr. Jamison releases you, we'll get you back. In the meantime, I think we all know who has to do some scouting." He looked at Cliff who nodded.

Rennin said to his old sensei, "We'll talk."

"Yes," agreed Cliff.

Rennin addressed the Council. "Let's adjourn until we have more information. I'll call a meeting soon."

Those present at the meeting disbursed. Laurel approached Aidan. "Hey, Island Boy. What's your plan?"

"To wait until I can make an informed decision."

"Well, you know I'm going back, right?"

"Yeah, I expect you to."

Her brows etched a deep V in her forehead. "I'm going with or without you."

"Yeah?" Aidan stretched his eyes wide. "What does that mean?"

She huffed, "I kind of thought you'd go with me."

"Why?"

Laurel folded her arms protectively across her chest. "Never mind."

"Do you need me to kill cockroaches since that's the only thing you're afraid of?"

She nodded vigorously. "Yeah. I might."

Aidan laughed loudly. "Can't you just admit you like me?" He held his thumb and index finger about an inch apart. "Just a little bit?"

She leaned in close. "Okay. I like you a little bit. But I really think you might be the catalyst to bring all the factions together."

"How can that be?"

She shrugged. "I don't know."

As they talked, Cliff made his way to them. He put his arm around his granddaughter. "Laurel, I need you to either stay with Ming or go back to Isla Linda with Aidan.

"Why, Grandpa?"

"I have a mission."

"You're going out there without me?"

"Yes, Laurel. And don't argue with me. Your doctor will sedate you if I ask."

Her mouth dropped open. "You wouldn't dare!"

"In a heartbeat."

Aidan guffawed. "Captain Moss, you've met your match." *Though I kind of hope that's me.*

Cliff grinned. "And if I go into combat, your commanding officer. Lieutenant colonel outranks captain."

Laurel's eyes narrowed to slits.

Cliff kissed her forehead. "And grandpa outranks granddaughter." He turned to Aidan. "Take her with you. I'm afraid she and Ming might cook up some sort of plan to follow me. Now, I have to get with Rennin and Char to plan this recon mission. Don't worry." He winked at his granddaughter. "In the immortal words of The Terminator—'I'll be back.'"

Laurel and Aidan watched as Rennin and Cliff sprang onto the backs of Smoke and Char and left.

Her face a puzzle, she looked up at the young man beside her. "Is he going alone?"

"No," said Aidan. "Char will be with him. Trust him, Laurel. Give those two a few weeks. Stevens won't be able to travel for at least six. Patience is a virtue."

"Yeah. One that I do not possess."

He wagged his head. "Well, I think I might try a little skiing. Want to come, or should I go without you?"

"I've never been on a pair of snow skis, only water skis."

"Time to learn." Aidan held out his hand. Reluctantly, Laurel took it. He led her to the flat place outside the cave entrance where he called, "Moonbeam, I need a lift."

7

Recon

In a cleft of a sheer granite face, Rennin O'Rourke, Clifton Spell, Char, Smoke, and Scarlet met to discuss a reconnaissance mission.

"Father, you should let me go with Cliff," Smoke intoned.

Shaking his huge black head, Char said, "No. He's my human."

"Mother, talk to him," Smoke argued.

"Your father's right," said Scarlet. "There will be no more talk about who's going."

"Good," said Cliff. "Char and I will do recon at night."

"And fly low, under radar," Smoke said. "Remember when we went to get d'Aubigné, Father. We showed up on their radar. They tried to shoot us down."

"I haven't forgotten, son," Char's gravelly voice said with calm.

"And, Cliff," Rennin put in, "you're not in the U.S. military anymore. We need to know exactly who we'll be opposing. I'm thinking at this point there are no good guys or bad guys."

"I understand that, Rennin."

"And if you can," Rennin continued, "see if you can find any we care for."

"No doubt. From what Laurel has said, Mom's Trading Post might still be intact. I'll definitely check there. I'll look for Margaret, the Pryors and the Muñoz family, oh, and Stephanie Pitts just for Gerald."

Rennin laughed. "You are just determined to goad him about falling for a younger woman and leaving her behind."

"If I find her, she won't be left behind."

Rennin clamped a hand on the other man's shoulder. "Just stay safe."

"Don't worry about us. We'll leave in the morning. Char is linked to Scarlet and Smoke. We'll send intel as fast as possible."

Early the next morning, Cliff and Char left with no one but dragon family and Rennin to see them off. Rennin felt it necessary to keep Laurel from knowing exactly when her grandfather would leave. He was certain she would insist on going with him even if she needed more time to heal. And the nagging notion that his own son would follow her spurred him to keep Cliff's departure secret.

The former military Black Ops officer and his bonded dragon flew along with minimal conversation. Once at the barrier that had not allowed passage for years, they waited and floated on gentle lapping waves. Nightfall would come shortly.

"Char, do you see anything?"

"No. It's too quiet for war."

"Could be the war is farther away."

"Yes, I suppose. Let's sleep until dark."

Cliff rubbed his friend's head. "You're okay with sleeping and floating?"

"Yes. Rest now."

A few hours later, Draconis's recon team crossed the barrier into the world of man. Char flew only feet above the water. A brilliant moon cast a soft glow making vision possible, even for the human.

After about a thousand miles, Cliff pointed to a shadow.

"What is it?" asked Char.

"Submarine—an underwater ship."

"Can they see us?"

"I don't know. We need to know who it belongs to."

"Should I dive?"

Cliff shook his head with a deep frown on his face. "No. If you showed up on radar, you'll show up on sonar."

"Sonar tracks underwater, right?"

"Yes."

"They might think I'm a whale."

"Doubtful."

Char twisted his head backward so that one eye looked at Cliff. "Then how can we figure out who owns it?"

"They're shallow. Let me dive. I'm small enough they won't think much of me."

"How long can you hold your breath?"

"No need." He pulled a wet suit from a large supply bag, then an oxygen tank. "I've had these on the yacht since we arrived nearly twenty years ago."

"Is it usable?"

"Yes. I checked it. Apparently, d'Aubigné's preservation spell kept more than the ship intact."

Cliff donned the diving gear. "I'll be back in a minute."

Char lowered a wing, and Cliff slipped noiselessly into the ocean.

Less than sixty seconds passed before Cliff surfaced. He climbed back onto Char. "British sub," he said. "I'm not certain where we are."

He pulled a compass from a duffle bag looped over one of Char's scales.

"Let's fly northwest. If we're in the Atlantic, we'll find land soon. If the Indian, we'll find land soon."

"Pacific?" Char chuckled.

"We might be seagoing for a while. But I think we're far South Atlantic, maybe even Antarctic Ocean. It's cold here. Winter in the southern hemisphere. With a British sub so close, we could be near The Falkland Islands."

They flew along over a large land mass without incident before the sun began to rise behind them. Then, they went over water again.

"Land," Char informed. "Maybe an hour."

Coming closer, Cliff said, "The Galapagos. Nice flying. We must have been in the Antarctic Ocean. We flew over the southern part of South America. We're in the Pacific now. I think we'll be fine here until night. Then, it'll be northeast." Cliff rubbed his head. "One reason Draconis has been so hard to find is that the fogbank changes location. Nice bit of magic. I can't help but wonder how long a vessel actually stays in the fog, maybe to be magically transported to a totally different area. It might seem like only minutes to people, but..."

"That would have been Alexander's enchantment. We can't ask him." Char observed, "I see no people or structures. Lots of turtles."

"Yep. Let's set down."

Their next rest stop put them in the Amazon Rain Forest. From their time over South America, the continent appeared relatively unchanged, though they did note a number of fenced camps and spotted many mutants within those enclosures.

"Refugees or prisoners?" Char asked as they took cover in the lush canopy.

"I think prisoners," said Cliff with a catch in his voice. "And those I fear are death camps. They can't cure them, so they kill them."

"Cliff, we have to stop it."

"We will once we get enough info. Send Scarlet what we've learned."

Another night of stealth flying brought the duo to South Florida. "Where do we hide today?" asked Char.

"Shit! There will be people—lots. The Everglades will be our best bet. You just stay out of sight. I'm going to find Margaret."

Char camouflaged himself beneath ancient cypress trees. "Look! Long-lost relatives." He chuckled at the multitude of alligators.

Cliff laughed. "Don't turn cannibal."

"I *am* getting tired of fish."

"You can probably find some deer while I'm gone. I'll be back soon."

Cliff hitched several rides until he found the address Laurel had given him. He took a steadying breath and knocked on the door. He turned his back and clasped his hands behind him in an at-ease military stance.

A petite older woman whose hair remained auburn tentatively opened. "Yes?"

Turning back, he said, "Margaret."

"Cliff?" Thereupon, she fainted.

A few moments later, Margaret Sanders opened her eyes. Clifton Spell smiled down at her where she lay on her own sofa. "Sorry to scare you," he said.

"I thought you were dead."

"Not quite."

"Where have you been?" Her voice sounded shaky.

"I'm glad you're lying down, or you might faint again." He then told her all about Draconis, about not getting her letter that they had had a child and grandchild until he couldn't get back, and finished by telling her Laurel was on Draconis.

"Dragons?" Margaret asked, thinking—*What kind of mushroom have you eaten?*

"Yes." He grinned at her dubious expression. "I'm not delusional."

"And you want me to go to Draconis?"

He nodded. "Soon. I think we'll need you here for a time to provide us with a base of operation.

"Dragons?" she said again, skepticism still evident in her voice.

"Yes, Margaret."

"Show me."

"You mean Char?"

"Did you bring more?"

"Not yet." He stood and held out his hand. "You drive."

Just edging on darkness the next day, Margaret parked at an overlook near The Everglades. Waiting for the one other car to leave, Cliff whispered, "Don't be afraid."

"Of course not. I could *never* be afraid of something that's going to eat the fifty pounds of pulled pork in my trunk." She giggled nervously.

Cliff chuckled. "He'd prefer it raw and still warm."

"Ewww." She crinkled her nose.

"Nobody should be coming now." He got out of the car and Margaret followed.

"Char!" Cliff called in a husky whisper. "Char!" he said a little louder.

Rustling toward the algae-covered water got their attention. A huge black snout and two golden orbs the size of basketballs hovered just atop the mossy water.

Margaret jumped back.

"Well, I see you found an excellent way to hide," Cliff said.

The gargantuan black beast pulled himself onto land. Margaret's mouth dropped open.

Cliff looked from human female to dragon. "Margaret, let me introduce Char. Char, this is Margaret Sanders."

"It's a pleasure," Char rumbled.

"You talk!" Margaret gulped.

"Yes."

"Oh, I don't believe it. I mean, I do, but..." She opened her trunk. "Are you hungry? We brought pulled pork."

Char sniffed the air, savoring the aroma. His chuckle shook the ground. "Cooked pig. Thank you. I'd rather have it raw, but I much appreciate your thought." Without another word, Char lapped every morsel from the three washtubs filled with food."

"It's a good thing we ate before," muttered Cliff.

"Oops. Sorry." Char licked his lips.

"Can I touch you?" asked Margaret.

"Of course." Char gave a nod.

Margaret ran a hand over his scales. "Amazing."

"Char," Cliff said, "Margaret thinks this could be a good place for us to base our operation. We can scout most of this country in two or three days. Then, fly over the Atlantic and see what we can in Europe and Asia with a hop to Africa and Australia. We should be able to gather a good bit of intelligence in two weeks, a month tops."

"Do we start tonight?"

"Yes. We'll go up the East Coast. West tomorrow."

"Um," Margaret said, "Cliff will sleep at my place during the day. Will you be all right here?"

"Yes," Char rasped. "I've made friends."

For the first time, the two humans noticed two dozen alligators. "Can you communicate with them?" asked Cliff.

"Yes, to an extent. They're very aware of all the bad things going on. Not only humans have died." Char looked toward his friends. "Margaret, would it be possible to bring chicken next time? One for each of them and, um, ten or twelve for me? Um, raw?" He clamped his teeth in a dragon smile.

"Sure." She nodded. *No way will I deny the request. I don't want to be eaten.*

For the next two weeks, Margaret fed more and more reptiles as Char and Cliff made numerous recon flights. She made sure Char let the alligators know that once he left, so would the free food.

While Margaret kept the alligators happy, Cliff and Char gathered valuable information.

The East Coast of the United States and Canada had tripled in population, but there seemed to be no contamination. Whispers in Washington talked of ridding the world of mutant beings, and a ripple expressed concern over the lack of the President's presence. The Vice President seemed to be handling affairs.

The Mid-west remained fertile land, as did the Gulf Coast area. Now and then a sick human would be found and shipped west to camps like the ones they had seen in South America. Cliff searched Mom's Trading Post, Pennsylvania, for loved ones, but if they were there, they were living under assumed names.

Crossing the Rockies felt as if a different world appeared. Cliff said, "I feel the radiation or some sort of oppression in the air."

"I'm taking you back," Char declared.

"Why?"

"What if the toxin is still in the air?"

"I doubt it is."

Char banked and forcibly set Cliff on the top of Pikes Peak. "I'll be back."

Shortly after sunrise, Char landed beside a still fuming Clifton Spell. He jumped to his feet and pointed. "You!"

"I'm responsible for you. I couldn't take the chance you would be exposed." Char pointed his own talon. "Now, sit so I can report."

Cliff sat down. Char started a small fire. Cliff pulled beef jerky and crackers from a pack, cocking an eyebrow at the dragon.

"I ate already," Char informed.

"You did?"

"Yes. There was a herd of large shaggy cows. I ate one."

"Buffalo."

"That's what they're called?"

Cliff nodded. "How many?"

"Hundreds."

"That's good." He nodded. "A resurgence of bison could be a good sign."

"Okay." Char dipped one eyelid in question.

"They were endangered, had low numbers."

"It seems they have multiplied."

Cliff rolled his hand. "So, report."

"Yes, of course. I also saw hundreds of those infected humans. Some seemed to be wild. There were others that showed evidence of organization. Parties hunted and a few appeared to till the soil."

Char settled into a comfortable position. "Rennin described a bridge. I think I saw it. That is where I saw the more structured groups. And the area that Rennin said would have been where the caves of gold once were seemed to house the structured groups—in the caves. They all disappeared out of the sun before it was very high in the sky." He blew a bit more fire onto the campfire. "I looked for the house of Peter Pryor. Those groups ran wild there. When any from that area approached the more organized ones, there was fighting. But sometimes, it seemed they communicated. And I observed a handful walking in the sun but wearing covering over all exposed body parts." Char yawned. "I also saw a few humans that looked perfectly normal, but they seem the most brutal of all."

Cliff scratched his head as he thought. Char offered one more tidbit. "There's an island with a large structure. I saw very organized but affected humans there."

"An island? Must be Alcatraz."

"Alcatraz?"

"Many years ago, it was a prison. Then, it closed, but tourists often visited. The government began letting them sleep there, almost like a bed and breakfast. It made money." He shrugged. "Report to Scarlet and rest. We need to get back to Margaret and then cross the ocean."

The two slept.

During the next week, Cliff and Char explored Europe and Asia. Cliff found the campground where Master Xing Tzu had stayed in the Himalayas. The memories of his first love and Ming's mother flooded him. His last visit there for Rennin to train under a master martial artist came back in a rush. This was the place he had been happiest before Draconis. No humans were around, so they made the deserted Tibetan tent village the base in that area.

From there, they viewed Western Europe, which seemed unscathed. Eastern Europe was not so lucky. Many infected humans roamed the Balkan area, but the heaviness of the air was less. Sarcastically, Cliff said, "It appears Transylvania is truly a land of monsters." Then he had to explain Transylvania and vampire and werewolf lore to Char.

In the former communist bloc countries, barbed- and razor-wire fences separated infected and non-infected humans. Cliff sighed as he watched. "These countries never seem to catch a break."

He took great note of the fact that non-infected humans scurried to enclosures before sunset. Infected humans rarely ventured out in daylight except occasionally on heavily cloudy days. Their eyes did appear to be covered with a film like cataracts, and their skin lost all color but for the frequent oozing, open sores. Darker skinned people seemed to have grayish pigment while Caucasians looked albino with white eyes.

Asia closer to the Pacific looked good, except for Korea, which was overrun with infected humans. The Middle East remained untouched by the bio-chem plague, but there was evidence of vicious fighting. Cliff shook his head. "Some things never change." Then he gave Char a history lesson on the Middle East.

The farther south they traveled in Africa, the more normal mankind became, though many more dictatorial chieftains seemed to flourish. Char's eyes widened and smoke escaped his nostrils as he witnessed atrocities against those who disagreed with the chieftains, atrocities that had gone on for hundreds of years he discovered after speaking with

Cliff. "Still," Char muttered, "it reminds me so much of the kinds of things Quazel did to the humans who would not worship her on Draconis."

They flew farther south. Australia looked to be a paradise.

Early on the twentieth day of their mission, Char and Cliff glided back into the safety of The Everglades. They waited until midnight when Margaret arrived with gator snacks.

"Margaret?" Cliff asked from the shadows.

"Oh! You're back." She flung cases of raw chicken into the marsh. Instant snapping could be heard.

She looked in the back of her car. "Char, I have three left. Need a little pick-me-up?"

The dragon bobbed his head affirmatively. Laughing, Margaret tossed the last three fowl into the air. Char gulped all three.

Cliff laughed. "You seem to have gotten comfortable with my best bud."

"Yes." She patted Char's tree-trunk-thick leg. "So, where to next?"

"We have to return to Draconis ASAP."

"I want to go too."

He gently touched her face. "Not yet. When more of us come to help out here, we'll need you here. As soon as this is over, I promise I'll take you with me."

Tears glistened on Margaret's cheeks. Cliff gathered her in his arms. "I promise."

"Cliff, can you ever love me?"

"I do. I just didn't realize it until it was too late. I have a second chance with you."

"Oh!" She touched his cheek.

He kissed her softly. "Take a ride with me."

Char held out a talon. Margaret grasped it and the dragon placed her on his back. Cliff climbed up behind her. They skimmed over the swamp, barely clearing the top of the cypress trees. "One day, we'll go higher," Cliff whispered in her ear.

Char landed by Margaret's car. Cliff kissed her once more and the dark duo winged toward home.

8

A Solution

Nearly half the residents of Draconis turned out to meet Cliff and Char upon their return. Laurel pushed her way through. Cliff embraced her tightly.

"How's my grandmother?" she demanded before, "I'm glad you got back safely."

Cliff chuckled. *Of course, her first priority would be Margaret.* He said, "Margaret is fine. She loves Char."

"Grandma actually met him?"

"Yes," Char rumbled. "She brought me pulled pork on our first encounter. Then, she fed the alligators while Cliff and I gathered information."

"What?" Laurel's eyes were as large as saucers.

"Lot's to tell," Cliff said.

"Father!" Smoke called, flying above the crowd.

"I'm fine, son," Char assured. "It was a most interesting experience."

Rennin called over the hubbub, "Cliff, Char, rest and visit with your loved ones. Day after tomorrow we'll meet to discuss your findings."

"Why not now?" Laurel griped.

Cliff put a hand on the impatient girl's shoulder. "We need time to replenish ourselves. Nothing will change in forty-eight hours."

Laurel argued, "More bombs."

Cliff shook his head. "The time for dropping bombs has passed. It's recovery time, but I fear most governments have sinister plans for recovery."

"What do you mean?"

"Destroying what cannot be fixed."

The Navy flier stretched her eyes wide. "Is there no other solution?"

"I think there is. We'll talk about it."

Char flew to his cave and devoured two cows, a goat, and a pig. Scarlet bustled around making sure his sleeping nook was perfect. Smoke and Moonbeam dropped in for a short visit, and then Char slept for the next two days.

Cliff visited with Ming and her family. Laurel stayed the night with her aunt and pried for information without success.

After a luscious dinner that Jacques prepared, Cliff kissed his daughter and grandchildren, bummed a lift from Filigree to his home in the mountains in the small village called Sierra Bluff and slept, himself, for a full day.

Knowing Char would need more down time than he did, Cliff asked Brindle to take him to Isla Linda to visit Laurel who had settled into a room at the O'Rourke home.

Flying over the island, he watched the granddaughter he had never been able to know catching butterflies in Morgan's Meadow with a young man who called him Uncle Cliff. To the perimeter of the park lay Moonbeam and Filigree. He chuckled. "Brindle, do you think that's two couples in the making down there? We know your granddaughter and Filigree are a done deal. What do you think about Laurel and Aidan?"

"I have no doubt they, too, will wed," the dragon droned softly.

"Really?"

"Yes. As much as her coming here has cast us into mayhem of another world, it also signifies the unity of the two worlds. She is meant for Aidan."

"His 'sunrise'?"

Brindle's laugh reverberated enough that both couples looked up. "No, Cliff, I think his tempest."

Cliff laughed with the dragon. "I agree."

Laurel waved to her grandfather. "Want me to pick them up?" Brindle asked.

"Why not?"

Brindle skimmed low enough to scoop the other two humans into gigantic talons, clenching them closed just enough to form two cages for safe transport. Moonbeam and Filigree headed back to the big island, playing roll and tag all the way there.

Hovering just out from the steps that led to the O'Rourke home, Brindle unloaded his precious passengers before he winged home.

Laurel engulfed her grandfather. "Grandpa! I want my own dragon, but Aidan says none of them would put up with my tempestuousness." She stuck her tongue out at Aidan.

Cliff roared with laughter. "Well, I suppose the solution could be to share Char."

"Oh, but I want Filigree."

"Oh, well. Is he bonded, Aidan?"

"Not that I know of, Uncle Cliff. He's pretty spoiled and childish himself."

"I am not childish!" Laurel snapped with accompanying foot stomping.

Shaking his head, Aidan said, "No, not at all."

Cliff kept chuckling. "Aidan, do you think Filigree would be interested?"

"Let's wait until everything is settled outside to ask."

"You're right," agreed Cliff.

"Darn it!" Laurel turned her lips into a pout.

"You know it's best to wait," Aidan said.

"Yeah, I guess." She turned to her grandfather. "How's Grandma?"

"Really good. When we go back, she'll help with a base of operations from her house and the dragons in The Everglades."

Laurel cocked an eyebrow. "So? You won't be helping with the military?"

"I might talk to some folks, but I cannot back what almost every government is doing with the people *they* infected."

"Which is?" Aidan asked.

"Almost everywhere we listened we heard whispers about mass extermination. They don't know how to cure them, so it's like putting down a rabid dog."

"But they're human," argued Aidan.

"Yes, but they have no idea how to help."

"And you do?" Aidan continued his inquiry.

"I might. We'll discuss it at Council tomorrow."

"Why the long wait, Grandpa?" Laurel asked.

"Char needs a great amount of sleep after such a long excursion."

"Really?"

"Yes. He can go quite a while with little rest, but when he crashes, he's down and out cold."

"Are all dragons like that?"

"Yes," Aidan informed.

"I see." She made a strange face. "So that would be their weakness. If too many were zonked, they could be attacked." She looked from man to man. "We have to protect them."

Aidan placed a hand on her shoulder. "You're catching on."

"Well," said Cliff, "I came just to visit. Any chance of a dinner invitation?"

"Sure, Uncle Cliff. Let me get busy."

"What's on the menu?" Cliff asked as they walked into the house.

"Stuffed flounder, cool ranch potatoes, and spinach salad. Ice cream for dessert."

"Yum."

Laurel laughed. "Grandpa, do any women on Draconis cook?"

Cliff chortled. "Yes, but there is little gender distinction on household chores. Renée has never been a good cook. You've met the twins by now. Both of them cook up a storm."

"Yes, I've met Caitlin and Morgan." *Yeah, and Island Boy let me think they were someone other than sisters, as well as Michelle Zane. I think he did it on purpose.*

Aidan grinned as he tuned into Laurel's pouty thoughts.

She said aloud, "Funny how they married brothers—Marshall and Randall Zane. Mr. Zane, Harvey, is cool, and his wife, Nicole, is awesome."

Cliff nodded. "She turned out so."

Grandfather and granddaughter plopped onto the sofa as Aidan headed to the kitchen. Cliff was surprised to see Lieutenant Stevens reading in a chair. "Hello, Lieutenant."

"You must be Lieutenant Colonel Spell. I've been anxious to meet you." The younger man stood and extended a hand, which Cliff shook.

The older man took stock of his granddaughter's navigator. *Well-toned muscle covers a solid six feet. He must be about the same age as d'Aubigné, but his dark hair already has signs of gray. Tough life. Yet, his brown eyes are alive.* "It's good to see you're recovering.

"Thank you, Sir. Dr. Jamison has cleared me for duty as soon as we know what we're going to do."

"I'm glad Laurel has you to back her up." *Wonder why they never hooked up other than rank.* "Do you have family to get back to?"

"No." The light in his eyes flickered. "No, Sir. My wife was a casualty of the bio-chem weapons."

"Sorry to hear it. My wife was murdered, but I have a new chance at love with Laurel's grandmother—even in my later years. Keep your heart open."

"I will."

"So, you're bunking with the O'Rourkes too?"

"Yes, Sir. They've been very hospitable."

"I'm sure they have. They're good people."

The visiting continued when Rennin and Renée returned from the big island over dinner and a few glasses of Rennin's home-distilled whiskey.

The next day, the Council met. Even after two days, Char was still sluggish, but functional. He would be himself after another good meal and a normal night's sleep.

Cliff wasted no time relating discoveries he and Char had made. When he got to the hushed plans of extermination, uproar began.

Craig Jamison sprang to his feet, his redheaded ire flaring. "Damn it! The medical community needs to be searching for a cure."

"Calm down, Craig," Rennin instructed.

Cliff said, "That's the first solution I'd like to propose. If we can determine exactly what was used on the victims, maybe we can formulate a cure—herbal and/or magical."

Heads nodded. "How do we do that?" Aidan asked.

Cliff looked around the group. "Some of us go into the other realm, bring back specimens and maybe procure some actual bombs. Analyze, experiment, and treat. It'll be tricky, but if somebody doesn't find a way to help—they're all dead."

Rennin addressed the Council. "Is there any dissention that this is our way of helping the outside world?" Much shaking of heads led to, "Then we need volunteers. No one will be asked or forced. This will be strictly voluntary."

Part Two

Gifts and Abilities

9

Jnto the Fray

Many came forward to plan Draconis's charge into the fray. Most native Draconians were assigned jobs to facilitate holding of specimens and to assist with research.

Craig Jamison and Renée O'Rourke set about designing a research facility. As soon as they had their ideas on paper, Tyler Bishop, d'Aubigné's husband, began the actual building to be located in the grassland of Prairieville.

At thirty-six, Tyler might have been the perfect specimen of a man—a solid six feet, etched muscles from years as a fisherman, sun-bronzed skin and light brown hair. His smoky blue eyes screamed that in no way would he fight and kill. His whole being exuded compassion.

Rennin put a hand on his son-in-law's shoulder. "When we bring some of the unfortunate people here, I want you to oversee their care. Get your two sisters-in-law to work as your caregiver team."

"Yes, sir."

"We both know d'Aubigné will necessarily have to work with Craig and Renée. Magic might be the only cure."

"When do the outside teams leave?"

"By week's end. Bring my daughter and granddaughter for supper tonight. Potluck. I'll do the pit barbeque."

"See you then."

The governor left.

That evening, Rennin's whole family came for dinner, along with a number of good friends.

Tyler and d'Aubigné showed up with their two-year-old daughter, Savannah, who already displayed magical ability and the tell-tale

O'Rourke green eyes and slightly pointed ears. They contributed a literal washtub of potato salad.

Aidan opened the door for them. "Wow, Sis! Are we feeding an army?" He smirked with mischief.

D'Aubigné squinted one eye while raising the other eyebrow in a high arch. "Actually, yes."

"I was teasing. This is all about who's to go where. Daddy's trying to do this with as little stress as possible. What better way than an O'Rourke feast? Did you send Draco to Morgan's Meadow? Daddy has the dragon munchies corralled there."

"Of course, I did. Are you going, Aidan?"

"Yes. I think I'm destined to have a huge role in ending this."

Tyler laughed. "And you don't want to lose track of your sunrise."

"That too."

D'Aubigné elbowed her husband's ribs. Savannah ran off to find playmates, which were available in abundance.

Aidan tipped his head. "You know where to find everyone."

"Yeah. Daddy's private park."

Aidan stepped out the door to walk with them. "Are we the last to arrive?" asked Tyler.

"Yep."

They walked around the side of the cave to which the house was attached to a large landscaped area with a pit barbeque and dozens of tables and chairs on a granite slab patio. Flowers bordered the floored area with an herb garden to one side and a smooth grassy area to the other. A large number of children of all ages played at various sports in this area. Savannah had found cousins and friends her age.

D'Aubigné caught sight of her twin sisters, Caitlin and Morgan, and went to greet them. The twins looked like their mother with blonde hair and blue eyes. They had married the Zane brothers, Caitlin to Marshall and Morgan to Randall. Caitlin and Marshall had two boys, Blake, three, and Drake, six months, both gingers like their grandmother, Nicole Zane, who could be seen across the way with more friends. Morgan and Randall had a daughter the same age as Savannah and were expecting another child. Rachel Zane was colored like her father and uncle with dark hair and eyes.

All the people who had come from the outside with Rennin years before were present with their families. For the first time, d'Aubigné's gut tightened as she realized the tranquil world they lived in was about to change forever.

As Tyler moved on to talk with Bobby Willis, a gorilla of a man who had stowed away with Cliff Spell's help to come to Draconis, the island's mage stopped to survey those she loved. Fear of losing any of them sent a shudder down her spine.

Jennifer Polson Willis, Bobby's wife and the woman who had been possessed by demons as a teen and tried to kidnap d'Aubigné and her sisters to be used as sacrifices, had become one of her closest friends. Jennifer and Bobby had three teenagers. D'Aubigné knew Bobby would follow her father to the ends of the earth, but Jennifer would never leave this place where she had found total healing and happiness except maybe to offer the solace she had found to others. There was truly not a violent bone in the woman's body.

D'Aubigné found her mother flitting around like the social butterfly she had always been. Casey McClarty Jamison sacrificed herself to save Rennin. Draco had met her on the path to eternity and sent her back to the land of the living. A hellion turned angel, Casey would never leave Draconis. She would stand by Craig's side until death.

D'Aubigné found her other brother, Colin, Casey and Craig's son. She laughed as she thought about his fiery temperament, much like his namesake, Colin Fitzpatrick, who had come from Ireland to Draconis centuries before. Just a few months older than Aidan, who would be going to war, Colin would stay here to defend the shores of his home unless necessity called him out.

Gerald McClarty's voice rang out, "Checkmate! I finally beat you!"

D'Aubigné turned her attention to her grandfather, the eldest person at the shindig. He stood and did a little victory dance as his former football protégé, Rennin O'Rourke, who had thought he was Troy Tomerson, chortled at his old coach's gloating for finally winning his second chess match against Cliff Spell. The two older men acted like The Odd Couple, but they were bosom buddies. Gerald would remain behind, but Cliff would be in the heart of battle if need be.

Harvey Zane raised his glass of Rennin's whiskey over his bald head. "A toast. To Gerald in his rare victory." Always referred to by his surname, Zane would go wherever Rennin went.

All present laughed at the good-natured jibe, raised their glasses of whatever beverage, and drank a toast.

Before she knew she was speaking, d'Aubigné called, "I foresee another victory—one of love."

All eyes turned her way. Not knowing what possessed her to speak, she blushed crimson. She went forward and hugged her grandfather.

Cliff Spell took her by the elbow a few minutes later. "What did that mean?"

"Stephanie Pitts. You bring her back to my grandfather."

"How do you know about her?"

"I don't know. It came to me in a flash of vision like Draco has."

At that thought, all the dragons who would be risking exposure, a way of life, flashed across her mind's eye.

"Uncle Cliff, we have to keep them safe."

"Them?"

They locked eyes. He nodded. No words were needed.

After a time of fun and food, all the adults, sixteen and older, sat down, sending the children to the game room; the time had come to give assignments.

Rennin stood and looked around his friends and family. "Only a few of us will go into the fray, at least initially. We will essentially work as insertion teams. Before we can do anything major, we need to bring back a good many humans that have been infected so Craig and Renée can determine exactly what we're dealing with. They, along with Tyler, have already begun a containment and research facility. It stands to reason that d'Aubigné will be called upon for many uses of magic before this is over." He winked at his firstborn.

"Caitlin and Morgan, I want you to help with caregiving when we get patients, and that's what they will be for us, not enemies, not prisoners."

The twins nodded their understanding. Their father went on. "Marshall, Randall, and Colin, just in case we end up fighting, I want you to train warriors while we're gone. You've all been trained in martial arts since you could walk. Now, we might have to fight. This is your mission.

"Jacques, I need you to work with any who wish to find a spirit guide. All of us going into the fray need to reconnect to our guides."

He looked around the group. "Any of you not given a specific task, stand ready to assist whoever might ask.

"Laurel and Dale, I suppose you'll have to report to your superior officers as a matter of honor. Cliff will visit Washington and try to speak with military leaders. Char will deliver the three of you to Miami and then transport Ming and Zane to the Himalayas where they'll be based. We need a good number of specimens from that area; and since apparently the first usage of what Lieutenant Stevens called bio-chem was by the North Koreans and Cliff and Char report the Korean Peninsula being overrun with bio-chem mutants, try to find unused weapons and chemical formulas. Those will help Craig and Renée find an antidote."

He ran a hand through still lush dark hair although the temples contained flecks of gray. "Moonbeam will take Aidan to Miami to await further instructions. He will stay with Margaret Sanders until Laurel and Cliff can relay an assignment. Moonbeam will be under the care of Char's friends in The Everglades and Margaret. I really think Aidan and Laurel will end up with, perhaps, the hardest mission. I'm not sure why.

"Smoke will take Bobby Willis and me to Mom's Trading Post. I'm hoping my old house will be empty. Bobby and I will search diligently for loved ones. Cliff may or may not join us. It will depend on his success with military leaders.

"Char, Smoke, and Moonbeam are blood relatives. They can communicate with one another and will have to be our message centers. Those of us bonded to them can communicate via thought to a lesser extent. We can relate emotion and silent calls for help. So, stay alert. If worse comes to worst, resort to using spirit guides."

He leaned on the back of the chair where his wife sat. She took both his hands in hers. He lifted her hand to his lips.

"Any questions?" Rennin asked.

Laurel raised her hand like a schoolgirl. "What's a spirit guide?"

Cliff informed, "It's an animal whose spirit has some connection to you. We've found our guides are able to manifest when we need them."

"Does everyone have one?"

Cliff shrugged. "Those more in tune with the spirit realm tend to find one."

"Spiritual realm, Grandpa?"

He nodded. "All warfare is ultimately spiritual."

"What's your guide?"

"A king scorpion."

She fidgeted. "How do I find my guide?"

"We don't have time right now for a vision quest."

"When do we leave?"

"Tomorrow morning at dawn," Rennin asserted.

10

◆ying ◆ow

Gerald McClarty insisted on bringing Cliff's yacht, *The Dragon Mara*; the *Spirit's Desire*, the vessel that had transported Rennin and Rebekah O'Rourke to Draconis; and *The Privileged Character,* which had been docked for over five hundred years, to the barrier. Somehow the old vessel was in as good a shape as the day she came to Draconis. He chose several Draconians to man the ships and wait for the first delivery of contamination victims. If the dragons left their specimens at the ships, they could return to the outside faster; and a good number of dragons remained behind to help if needed.

Rennin couldn't argue with the logic, so three ships anchored to wait and three dragons with passengers flew beneath radar straight to Miami.

Laurel chose to ride with Aidan on Moonbeam. Arriving at The Everglades well after dark, the three dragons slipped into the water and Cliff pulled out a cell phone—the tiniest any of the humans from Draconis had ever seen.

"Margaret gave it to me to contact her when I got back," Cliff explained at the amazed expressions on their faces. He, then, dialed her number, and she arrived forty-five minutes later driving a large van and delivering three heaping washtubs of raw ground beef. The three dragons scarfed it down and returned to hide in the marsh.

The humans climbed into the vehicle after Laurel and her grandmother had an emotional reunion. They crashed at Margaret's house until the next day.

Mid-morning, Cliff, Laurel, and Stevens headed to Washington D.C., in Margaret's car. Laurel and Stevens had donned their uniforms.

The drive from Miami up the East Coast was strained. The two younger people knew once they reported, they might be given another military assignment.

Cliff suggested, "Ask for leave since you crashed and need more time to recover." He handed both of them a tiny vial containing a yellow powder. "If they don't grant your request, dump this into your palm and blow it into their faces. They'll be putty in your hands for half an hour, just long enough to get your request in writing. They won't remember a thing."

"What is it, Grandpa?" Laurel asked.

He grunted, "It's best you not know."

"Drugs?" asked Stevens.

"Magic," Cliff stated.

They arrived at the Pentagon and gained entrance after much haggling over Cliff.

The guards on duty allowed Captain Moss and Lieutenant Stevens entry without incident but argued while pointing at a computer screen. "Lieutenant Colonel Clifton Spell is presumed dead."

"Do I look dead?" Cliff snapped.

"No, Sir, but you've been missing for almost twenty years."

"Just because I chose to go and live away from civilization—which doesn't seem so civilized—doesn't mean I died. Who reported me missing?"

"I don't know."

"Are you going to let me pass, or do I need to resort to drastic measures?"

"You aren't armed."

Laurel and Stevens waited on the other side of the guard station. She hissed at the guard, "He doesn't need a weapon. He's a master martial artist and could kill you with his bare hands."

Cliff shook his head. "I'm not here to kill anybody."

Feeling his hand forced, he took out his own vial and dumped the contents into his palm. The guard who had been talking took the safety off his weapon and aimed at Cliff's head.

Cliff laughed outright and blew the powder into the two men's faces. Instantaneously, they became almost incoherent. "Holster your weapons," he said, and they complied. Cliff led the guard who had drawn the gun to the log-in. "Indicate you allowed me to pass." The guard did. Cliff joined his granddaughter and Stevens.

"So, that's what the powder does," surmised Stevens.

"Yep. Now, Rennin has no need for the powder. He just has to wave his fingers, and the weak-minded are his to control."

"Like a Jedi knight?" Stevens asked.

"Exactly," Cliff replied without further explanation.

The three walked on.

Once inside the building, Laurel and Stevens went straight to the office of Admiral Sylvester Bolton. The white-haired man said, "We have you listed as MIA. What happened, and where have you been?" He pointed at two chairs. "Sit and talk."

"We crashed, Sir," Laurel said as she sat down, "on an uncharted island. There was no way to communicate." Stevens sat beside her.

"We found some wreckage. I thought you two were dead."

"Wounded. Stevens more so than myself. There were a few people there, and they nursed us to be well enough to get back, but we both need more recovery time. We're requesting leave."

"You don't look too hurt right now."

"Internal injuries take more time, Sir."

He scrutinized the two. "Could it be that you're just tired of the fighting and want out?"

"Sir, we will do our duty."

"And if I don't grant your leave?"

Laurel took a deep breath and felt the vial in her pocket. She decided to try one more approach before using its contents.

"Sir, one of the people on this island was my grandfather, Lieutenant Colonel Clifton Spell."

The Admiral sat forward. "Cliff is alive?"

"Yes, Sir."

"What is he up to, taking two of my best?"

"I didn't say…"

"You don't have to. I know the man. I'm thinking he's got a plan for the poor devils who were hit with bio-chem. Where is he?"

"Looking for the Joint Chiefs of Staff."

"Can you contact him? He's wasting his time."

Laurel retrieved another tiny cell phone her grandmother had provided and called her grandfather. Ten minutes later, he entered the room

Admiral Bolton stood. "You old dog! I thought you were dead."

The two shook hands. Cliff said, "Very much alive and kicking. Good to see you, Sly."

"What's your plan?" He indicated another chair, and Cliff sat.

"Well, I'd like to get some of the bio-chem victims and take them back to my island. Do a little research. Maybe find an antidote."

"Some black magic, voodoo, mumbo-jumbo, I'll bet."

Cliff glared at the man he had known more than half his life.

Admiral Bolton continued, "Talking to the assholes upstairs won't help. They're planning the use of napalm on any settlement they come across, and they've got other countries on board with them. They want to eradicate the mess they've made and start over. My hands are tied. They haven't listened to me."

"Can you buy us six to eight weeks?"

"No promises, but I'll try. I'm assigning you these two. Do what you can. Keep me informed." He signed an order for Captain Moss and Lieutenant Stevens to be on a covert assignment and sent the three packing with a final comment. "If your mission succeeds, I'll sign your military releases, Moss, Stevens. Honorable discharges with meritorious service."

While the trio was in D.C., Char transported Ming and Zane to the Himalayan tent village where Ming had spent her early years. They did more recon with Char. When they returned to the village, the two humans began building bamboo cages to hold six.

Ming rubbed Char's shiny scales. "Find us some food. You should be able to find gorals and yaks easily. Once we get these built, you'll have a tougher assignment."

As they worked in Asia, Smoke discreetly landed Rennin and Bobby on the banks of Beaver Creek in front of the house Rennin had owned in Mom's Trading Post.

It had fallen into disrepair again, but the dragons painted on the house looked as if they had been done the day before. The house appeared uninhabited.

Rennin said, "This looks good, Bobby. Smoke stay close to the creek. Dive if you need to. We're about to check out the house."

On the veranda, Bobby pointed to the broken lock. Rennin nodded. "Looks as if someone has been here."

Rennin opened the door. *WHOMP!* A baseball bat went across his middle. He doubled over with a groan.

"Rennin!" Smoke charged the door, wedging just his snout in behind his bonded human, smoke curling from his nostrils. Bobby still stood on the porch.

The people inside screamed in panic and scurried deeper into the house.

"Stop!" an authoritative voice rang out.

A hoary-headed man knelt beside the downed man. "Rennin O'Rourke, a.k.a. Troy Tomerson?"

"Yeah," he wheezed out and looked up with only his emerald eyes. "Peter?"

The older man embraced Rennin in a bear hug.

11

As Many as Possible

Peter Pryor helped Rennin stand. "I'm sorry. We've had a little trouble with folks trying to get to Stephanie, and what is that thing?"

"Who?" Rennin was finally able to get his breath. Smoke withdrew his head from the door and went back to the creek. Bobby stepped inside.

Bobby snickered. "That *thing* is a dragon."

Peter shook his head as if to dislodge something. "A what?"

"Dragon," Rennin reiterated.

"You always said they were real."

"Yep."

"Okay, I'll come to grips with that in a minute." Then he explained their situation. "Stephanie Pitts escaped with us. She's infected, but not when we left San Francisco. As we crossed the river into Colorado, a seriously infected human bit her hand. We couldn't draw attention to ourselves, so we just pushed the mutant away and hauled ass. Her symptoms started around Oklahoma. We keep her contained in a room upstairs. It's so sad to see her. It's like she's trapped inside. She tries to communicate and can't. That's when she starts slapping her head and crying."

Rennin's eyes stretched. "So, she's not like a zombie or cannibalistic?"

"No."

"May I see her?"

"Sure." Peter eyed the younger man with his godson. Rennin made the introductions, and Peter waved Bobby into the living room and took Rennin up the stairs. He unlocked the padlock on the door.

"Stephanie, you have company," Peter said.

Rennin remembered the pretty brunette who was close to his age. Her blue eyes were vacant, skimmed over. She sat passively in a chair in the room. At the sound of her name, she turned her head toward Peter.

He continued to speak. "It's Rennin O'Rourke. Do you remember him?"

She worked her mouth, desperate to speak. Rennin popped his hand over his mouth and had to stifle tears. Finally, she eked out one word. "Help."

Rennin knelt in front of her and took her hand. "Stephanie, I'm going to ask you some questions. If you understand, squeeze my hand."

He felt pressure on his hand.

"Okay, now answer yes with two squeezes; no with one. Do you understand?"

He felt two distinct squeezes.

"Were you infected in San Francisco?"

He felt one hard squeeze. Rennin looked at Peter.

"Her infection is much less severe than most," Peter offered. "I really think it happened when she got bitten."

"Residual poisoning?"

He felt two squeezes.

Rennin smiled. "Do you believe in magic?"

He felt two less firm squeezes. He took it to mean she might be a little skeptical.

"If I could send you somewhere to get help, would you go?"

Two bone-crushing squeezes met his hand.

"Even if a dragon takes you?"

She made a noise but squeezed twice.

"About that dragon," Peter began. "Damn! They're real."

"Yes," assured Rennin. "The one outside is called Smoke."

"The same Smoke from *Memoirs of Magic*?" Peter's voice sounded higher than normal.

"Yep. Listen, Draconis is real. Some of us, including three dragons, have come to collect infected people to take back and look for an antidote. We want to get as many as possible. Stephanie, Peter says there are those much worse off than you. It could be that they got a higher dose of bio-chem, but it's present in their saliva. Will you go so Dr. Craig Jamison can draw some blood and begin research?"

She squeezed his hand tightly twice.

"Good," he said. "Gerald McClarty is there."

"J-j-j," came from Stephanie's mouth as her lips curled into a smile.

Rennin patted her leg. "He kind of likes you too."

He turned to Peter. "How have you been surviving? Did you get the water and electricity turned on here?"

"No, we've been squatters living off the grid. The creek is right here. We've used the firepit and grill out back for our cooking."

"Were you here a few weeks ago?"

"We've been here nearly a year. After we left our car, we walked the rest of the way. When we saw Stephanie's change, we were forced to travel at night. But no way would we abandon her. She would have been shot on site so far from the containment zones."

"But Cliff didn't find you."

"So, that was Clifton Spell. We didn't know who he was, so we stayed hidden."

"Well, I'm here to take folks back. Do you want to go?"

Peter nodded. "But not until I see some change here. Get Stephanie there, and we'll stay here to help you."

"Okay. I might need some help."

Rennin stood and went to talk to Smoke. He explained what was happening.

"Perhaps Aidan and Moonbeam could come and get her," Smoke suggested.

"Good idea. Have you heard anything from Char?"

"They're building containment pens. I'll send what we're doing. You call Aidan on that—phone."

Near morning, Aidan and Moonbeam arrived. They would need to rest and wait for nightfall. Peter's family relaxed and got to know two dragons and young men they had never met before. Peter liked both young men and was impressed with Aidan's maturity, and he told them so. He chuckled. "Rennin, he's a lot more grown up than seventeen. A lot more serious than you were at that age."

Rennin nodded. "Yes. I was a brat, even if I was poor. Eva spoiled me as far as she could. Aidan, has his mother's temperament."

"I think she's a bit hotheaded as I recall, and definitely stubborn," Peter argued. "I bet Aidan inherited Duncan's spirit."

"I agree," Smoke said with a dragon grin.

Aidan laughed at his father's annoyed expression. "If I inherited the spirit of Duncan O'Rourke, I'm honored," the youngest O'Rourke intoned.

They visited a bit longer while Aidan ate and then slept.

At dusk, Peter and Rennin led Stephanie out to meet Smoke and Moonbeam. She balked for a moment. Moonbeam held out her open talon. Stephanie looked toward Peter. Though a fine film covered her eyes, her pupils were wide with fear. Her dragon ferry whispered, "It's okay. Come on."

Stephanie reached out a tentative hand. Moonbeam scooped her up and formed a safety cage with her talon, pulling it close to her chest.

Aidan and Rennin embraced, and then Aidan swung onto Moonbeam's back. They took off, flying low.

Around midnight, they met Margaret at The Everglades. Moonbeam set her wary passenger down. Aidan sprang from the dragon's back and took Stephanie's hand.

He said, "We'll sleep at Margaret's today and go on tomorrow evening. We'll rendezvous with Grandpa Gerald."

"J-j-j." Stephanie struggled to speak.

Margaret touched Stephanie's shoulder. "Come on, sweetheart. I'm Margaret Sanders. I'll take care of you. Would a hot bath make you feel a little better?"

Stephanie nodded.

Margaret cared for the younger woman as she would a daughter.

At breakfast, more evidence of her contamination became apparent as she could not hold a fork or spoon. She resorted to eating like an animal.

Having a strong gift of empathy, Aidan felt her distress. He put aside his utensils and gobbled his bacon and eggs directly from the plate.

Tears filled Margaret's eyes. She feared the same fate could befall Laurel. She sat beside Stephanie and followed Aidan's example, eating from her plate without utensils.

Tears dripped down Stephanie's cheeks. "Th-thnk."

Aidan took her hand. "No thanks necessary."

When it came time to leave, Stephanie climbed into Moonbeam's talon without fear. They flew to the far South Atlantic and came upon a dense fog bank. Once they exited the fog, they spotted Cliff's yacht.

Moonbeam lowered Stephanie, and Aidan jumped onboard the ship. Gerald McClarty ran to the deck, his heart in his throat as he recognized a much younger woman that he had developed feelings for many years before but had never voiced them or acted upon them.

"I'm sorry, so sorry I left you. Please forgive me," he begged.

"J-j-j," was all she could manage.

Aidan hugged the man. "Grandpa Gerald, Moonbeam is summoning Scarlet. Let her take Stephanie to Draconis so Momma and Uncle Craig can begin research."

Within the hour, Scarlet arrived and took charge of their refugee. Gerald kissed her forehead and sent her to seek healing.

Aidan and Moonbeam rested and waited for darkness before they winged back to Miami, being sure to fly low enough not to be detected.

In the Himalayas Ming and Zane, armed with sleeping-compound darts, began their stealth missions. With Char's ability to snatch prey on the move, by week's end, they had two dozen bio-chem victims from Asia and Europe, half being from Korea.

Char sent Scarlet a telepathic message for assistance. Then, Ming insisted on a few more victims from other places. She and Char hit North Africa while Aidan and Moonbeam collected a few more from South America. Those there proved to be mostly from elsewhere. Apparently, South American countries were paid to house severely infected victims.

By the end of the second week, Scarlet, Esmeralda, who was Draco's mate, and Filigree arrived at the Tibetan camp to transport the victims. Ming and Zane had grouped them by severity of affliction, but all were much worse than Stephanie.

Once the patients were delivered, three new dragons joined Char. They chose to stay in the mountains because their vibrant colors would be hard to camouflage. Scarlet looked just as her name indicated. Esmeralda resembled a giant Luna moth with her florescent green scales. Filigree's name also suited him, as his scales appeared as golden shields over his body.

During this time, Cliff, Laurel, and Stevens had disappeared to a secluded spot in the Shenandoah Valley. Laurel begged for a vision quest and ordered Stevens to participate.

After days of vision quests with the two, Stevens grinned. "I don't mind being a bull elephant. I already knew I had a memory like an elephant. My spirit guide is awesome."

"Oh, shut up!" Laurel folded her arms across her chest.

"Why? Were you a shrew?"

Cliff broke into laughter.

"No." She sighed. "I was an albatross. I read *The Rime of the Ancient Mariner.*"

Cliff put his arm around her. "Then you should know that they're lucky, and the bad luck that befell the ship was because one of them killed an albatross. And"—He squeezed her against him—"albatrosses mate for life."

She asked, "What's Aidan's spirit guide?"

He let her go and almost couldn't breathe he laughed so hard. Through gasps, he said, "Are you hoping he's an albatross to mate with?"

"That's not what I said," she spat out.

"Stop fooling yourself, little one." He sobered. "No, Aidan's guide isn't an albatross, but it does mate for life. I'll let *him* tell you.

"Now, we have to get to Miami. You and Aidan have a big mission. Stevens has to go back to Draconis. He has military expertise to share."

They sped back to find Aidan perfectly at home with Margaret. He shared with them about Stephanie Pitts.

Cliff clapped the young man on the shoulder. "Well, tomorrow you, Laurel, and Moonbeam start a mission."

"What is it?"

"Getting to the West Coast undetected and bringing back some victims. That area is heavily guarded, not like some other countries. I have all the gear you'll need. Char needs to come and take Stevens back to Draconis and I need to join Rennin. Admiral Bolton is buying us some time. Now, let's rest. I'm pooped."

12

Empathy

The next evening was upon them before they opened their eyes. All parties congregated at The Everglades. Moonbeam informed the lot, "Grandfather will be here by dawn. He'll do whatever Cliff asks. What are we to do?"

Cliff set about explaining the equipment. Laurel interrupted her grandfather. "I know how to use gas masks and bio-suits."

"Aidan doesn't."

She glanced at the young man who would be going with her to the hardest hit area in the Americas. *God! I'd hate for anything to happen to that body. He is so gorgeous.*

Aidan gave her a pouty, seductive smile, as if he'd read her mind.

She shivered and said, "Sorry. I forget you're new to this stuff."

"I think I've got it, though," Aidan said, still grinning. He picked up a hand-held Geiger counter. "This machine will let us know if the radiation level is safe. How do we know if the biological and chemical levels are safe? If we have to wear protective clothing, we won't be so unnoticeable."

Cliff handed him another gauge. "I'm assured this will indicate any dangerous particles in the air."

"What about Moonbeam?"

"I'm pretty sure dragons might be impervious to all but direct hit or massive levels of radiation; and from what I could discover, only humans and higher primates seemed affected by bio-chem. Laurel has said that limited exposure in the irradiated areas is possible for humans. Moonbeam will be fine."

"Are you sure no other mammals were affected?"

"Well, not residually. Only by first contact, and that seemed to be instant death."

"Okay, Uncle Cliff." Aidan took a deep breath. "So, what's the plan?"

Cliff spread out a map with areas highlighted. "The orange areas seem to be greatly infected. Observations show the collectives here to be feral. Craig has sent word he'd like at least two dozen specimens from here. Construct containment pens that Moonbeam can get to The Everglades. Char will transport them from there. Randall and Marshall Zane will be joining Margaret to help take care of things here."

He pointed to a block. "This is the area where your father lived."

"That's Puma Pass?" Aidan asked for confirmation of which place his father had lived since Rennin had also lived in Miami before Puma Pass, California, and Mom's Trading Post, Pennsylvania, afterward.

"Yes. Here in the caves and here on Alcatraz appear to be groups of very organized infected beings. We need to know how and why they function at such a higher level. We want two dozen of them too."

Cliff opened one last small box. He held up two contact lens cases. "I think the people in Puma Pass are highly capable. From what I saw, their minds have not been altered. These are contact lenses to make your eyes appear clouded. You might have to infiltrate them."

Aidan and Laurel took the cases. Cliff reminded, "We're working on borrowed time. Get busy." He kissed Laurel's cheek and hugged Aidan. Last he gave a pat to Moonbeam's side. "Take care of them."

The dragon bobbed her large head in affirmation as a swirl of smoke rose from her nostrils.

As Moonbeam flew silently over half a country, Laurel watched intently through infrared goggles. "Aidan," she said, "I don't like what I see."

"Talk to me."

"We've made a point of flying over several military installations. I've noticed a stockpile of rockets, and Grandpa mentioned plans for using napalm to eradicate people who were infected."

"Explain this napalm to me. I felt stupid asking before."

"You understand what gasoline is, right?"

"Yes. I think so. You need it to make your cars run, and it's flammable."

"Right. Napalm, also called a firebomb fuel gel mixture, has a gel-like consistency, allowing it to stick to targets. It's often used in combination with gasoline or jet fuel—that's for airplanes—to make a bomb with a thin outer shell that easily explodes and ignites upon impact with a target."

"So? Basically burning these defenseless people alive?"

"Yeah." Laurel sighed.

"You think we have less time than we thought?"

"Maybe."

Moonbeam groaned. "Do we change plans?"

"No," Laurel said. "Just stay vigilant in case we have to do something quickly."

"All right." The dragon landed with a thump in an area on Pikes Peak. "This is the camp Grandfather mentioned."

"How do you know?" asked Laurel.

"I smell him and Cliff." She blinked golden eyes with stick-like lashes.

Laurel rolled her eyes. *How dumb of me.* "Of course," she said aloud.

The two humans slipped off Moonbeam's back. Aidan yawned. He looked to the east. "It's close to dawn. We need to rest."

They set about making camp. Moonbeam started a fire. Aidan pulled out rations and began a meal.

Moonbeam's eyes darted about. "I'll be back in a jiffy."

Before either human could object, she zoomed away. She returned within half an hour.

"Where did you go?" demanded Laurel.

"Breakfast." Moonbeam set her teeth in a dragon smile. "There were a number of bears just down the slope."

"You just ate a bear?"

"Two."

Aidan chortled. "Moonbeam has to eat, Laurel."

"I know, I know." She waved her hands in the air. "It just takes getting used to."

"Just so you know, I made sure not to eat babies or mothers." Moonbeam nodded, pleased with her idea of conservation. "Actually, I think it was two males about to fight." Her mouth stretched wide in a yawn. She curled up near the fire and wrapped her wings around her. Within minutes, buzzing sounds and wisps of smoke emanated from the beast.

Laurel shook her head while Aidan rehydrated powdered eggs and stirred them in a camp skillet, serving two plates with jerky and individually wrapped bread slices. Laurel took the food.

Aidan asked, "What has you disoriented?"

Laurel pointed. "She just drops to sleep anywhere."

"I guess she feels safe enough. Not too much can hurt a dragon, though I do worry about rockets and missiles. And we know they can be harmed by magic."

"So far, so good." Laurel sighed and sat on the ground beside Aidan. They ate and then prepared to sleep.

Laurel wrapped in the thermal sleeping bag her grandfather had secured and still complained, "I'm cold. I'm from Florida and used to a ship with temperature control."

Aidan chuckled. "Is that your way of asking to share a sleeping bag?"

"What?" She glared at her companion.

"Oh, come on, Laurel! You're cold. Come over here and snuggle with me to stay warm. Use your bag as an extra blanket over us." He unzipped his bag and held it open. "I'm not going to touch you inappropriately." He sniggered. "Unless you want me to." *And you do want me to. I feel it.*

"Oh, shut up." She gathered her bag, slipped in beside Aidan, and arranged her bag over them as a blanket.

Aidan zipped them in and spooned against her. "Better?"

"Yeah. You're comfy."

He kissed the back of her head. "Sleep, Sunrise."

"Okay, Island Boy."

No argument. Aidan grinned and fell asleep.

Sometime during slumber, Laurel and Aidan changed positions a number of times. Moonbeam's throaty, "Ahem," woke them. They were entangled, and their lips touched as their eyes popped open.

"Sorry," Aidan intoned and began disengaging their wrapped bodies. *Not really.*

"No problem," Laurel muttered.

As they took care of personal needs, Aidan grinned. *She's smiling. She liked being beside me. Yes, indeed. My Sunrise.*

Again, he made a quick meal. He was looking at the map when Laurel came to the campfire after cleaning up. "San Diego seems to have a huge population of less functional creatures," he said.

"Makes sense they'd target a naval base."

"Let's get several pens built and tomorrow we'll put Moonbeam's talents to good use and snatch a few. She'll whisk them to Miami, and we'll stay here and do the same thing to Los Angeles when she returns. Think you'll be safe with me without a dragon?"

"I'm not afraid of you." Laurel picked up a hatchet. "Let's get to work."

Moonbeam stretched her talons wide open. Razor-sharp claws extended, just like a cat. "I have a better idea. This way we can get specimens from both places tonight."

Using spruce saplings, heated pine tar courtesy of Moonbeam, and strong hemp rope, they had five eight-by-eight cages constructed by nine. Moonbeam grinned and blew on her finely-honed claws.

"Makes short work of skinny little trees, huh?"

Laurel chuckled. "I must confess my appreciation for your talons."

"Now, should I find us some people?"

"Yes," said Aidan.

"Be back in a flash." The dragon swooped downward in a graceful arc.

"That's so beautiful," murmured Laurel when glow from the rising moon reflected off scales of quicksilver.

"Yep. She is," said Aidan.

Hour after hour, Moonbeam brought humans with clouded eyes, extended frontal lobes, stooped posture, constant touching of the opposite gender's genitalia, and hyper aggression by a male once he laid claim to a female. Still, they communicated via grunts and their fear of Moonbeam, unaffected humans, and being confined was palpable. Their terror made Aidan clutch his heart, pain radiating through his entire body.

"Aidan!" Laurel screamed.

"I'm okay. Let me try to calm them." He tried any number of ways. Offerings of food and music seemed most effective.

He muttered, "Music sooths the savage soul. Turn up the music a little, Laurel."

She increased the volume of the portable CD player she had in her pack. Vivaldi's *The Four Seasons* wafted on the air.

Aidan passed dried fruit through the bars.

Laurel scolded, "Aidan, you'll give away all our provisions."

Handing jerky to a boy about his age, he said, "We'll get more, or Moonbeam can hunt for us."

As he spoke the dragon came in with one more human grasped protectively in her talons. The boy pointed and jerked Aidan's arm through the bars. "Uh! Uh!" he grunted, an iron grip on the other's arm.

"Moonbeam won't hurt you," Aidan assured in a soft, cooing voice. "We want to help."

"He doesn't understand you, Aidan," Laurel said, exasperation weighting her voice.

"Yes, he does." Aidan pried the boy's hand from his arm and motioned for him to stand back.

The boy knitted brows of a slightly protruding forehead and stepped back. Moonbeam gently pushed a young, obviously pregnant, girl into the enclosure. The girl screamed. The boy grabbed her and put her behind him."

"Good, Lord!" exclaimed Aidan. "She's pregnant."

Moonbeam nodded. "I thought Craig would really like that. They can reproduce."

The boy grunted again, his arm around the expectant mother's shoulders.

"Oh," Aidan whispered. "Laurel, come here. Please, just go along."

Laurel came to Aidan. "What?"

Aidan put his arm around her and planted a kiss on her. She pushed back. "Stop," he whispered. "That's his mate."

Aidan turned to the captive couple. He pointed from himself to Laurel. "Mate."

The boy bobbed his head, knelt, and put his hands on the girl's abdomen.

Aidan said, "Baby," and held his arms in a cradle-lock, rocking them back and forth.

"Baa-bi," the boy sounded out.

"Yes." Aidan nodded and then touched his chest. "Aidan."

The boy's scowl deepened. Aidan touched Laurel's chest. "Laurel."

"Ay-in. Lo-lo." The boy mimicked Aidan's motions. "Si-am. Ma-ri."

"Sam? Mary?"

The boy nodded.

Aidan pointed to his bonded dragon. "Moonbeam."

Sam stood straight from the hunched position he had been in. A slow head shake preceded, "Dragon."

13

Inherited Memory

"**Yes!**" Aidan shouted in unrestrained excitement. "How did you know? Oh, you can't answer. Moonbeam, did you tell him?"

"No." The massive beast wagged her head.

"Uh!" Sam stuck his hand through the slats of the cage.

Aidan took his hand. Sam pulled Aidan against the bars. Both Laurel and Moonbeam tensed when Sam forced their heads to touch.

A few minutes later, Aidan stepped back—a million thoughts and images flashing through his mind. "Oh, Jesus. Help me, Lord." Weak-kneed, he sank to the ground and looked up at Sam. "Can you do that with everyone?"

Sam shook his head. "Empth."

"Empath? Only with an empath?"

Sam nodded.

Laurel blurted, "You're an empath?"

Aidan confessed, "I have some ability to sense mood and emotion. This isn't about me. These people who were residually affected haven't degenerated mentally, only in the ability to communicate and control emotional impulses. On the contrary, their mental capacity has been heightened. Their thoughts are trapped within, much like an autistic person. He gave me a huge list of symptoms. I'll write them down and send them to Uncle Craig."

Aidan turned back to Sam. "We're here to help. You saw my mind too. You know I speak truth. Will you go with Moonbeam, work with your people, and help find a cure?"

Sam touched Mary's baby bump again.

Aidan held up a hand in oath. "I swear we'll keep both of them safe. You'll be better off on Draconis, no matter."

Sam nodded.

"Time is of the essence here. Moonbeam, lean down." When she did, Aidan touched the sides of her head in the soft space just behind her eyes. He transferred Sam's images to her.

"What did you do?" asked Laurel.

Aidan blushed. "I gave her what Sam gave me. Uncle Craig, Mom, d'Aubigné, or someone else can retrieve them."

"Telepathy?"

"In a way. If your spirit isn't receptive to the dragon's spirit, it won't work."

"Okay. Let me try."

"If you insist, but don't force it." He stepped back and waved her forward.

Laurel touched Moonbeam with trembling hands.

"Relax," whispered the dragon.

The girl placed her hands as Aidan had. After a few minutes, Laurel fell to the ground, unconscious.

"I'm sorry," Moonbeam whined. "I didn't mean to."

"What happened?" Aidan demanded, dropping to his knees beside the girl.

"I couldn't control it. All the inherited memory just shot out. I tried, but it just poured out. She saw *everything*."

"From Quazel on?"

"Before even."

"How?"

"Because…because she's descended from Alexander too!"

"What? How?" Aidan poured water on a bandana and washed Laurel's face.

"It goes back to Michael O'Rourke, Gabriel's twin, born in Puma Pass. He didn't believe Draconis was real."

"I remember that from reading old journals. He joined the Navy and moved to Miami. He died during the Spanish-American War."

Laurel moaned a bit but did not rouse.

Sam held tightly to the bars, a hint of blue flashing through the cataract-like coating.

Moonbeam went on. "Yes, and he had no sons for the O'Rourke name to continue through him, but he did have daughters."

Her tail thumped in excitement. A small trembling shook the mountain. "You and Laurel share a great-grandfather."

"How?" Aidan's voice reverberated from peak to peak.

"Yes. Well." A tiny spark shot from Moonbeam's mouth. "Oh! Cliff! Cliff's mother! She wasn't a prostitute at all. She was a descendent of Michael and an empath. Her ability makes yours look silly. They said she was schizophrenic, that she heard voices. She was in an asylum. She escaped. She had a baby. She did commit suicide, but she left her child with the Catholic Church.

"Oh, Draco, Grandfather, even Grandpa pursued her. They were ready to accept a female descendent without the O'Rourke name. When she told others about the dragons, they thought she was stark raving mad."

She shook her head. Large dragon tears dripped to the ground. Steam rose from them. "Oh! They felt so guilty about her. Your grandfather and great-grandfather believed some, but their spirits were not strongly connected. Then, Rennin was born, and from birth was connected."

"Moonbeam!" Aidan clenched his fist. "You're rambling. How do we share a great-grandfather?"

"Sorry. As much as my mind is racing, Laurel must be in mental overload."

"Moonbeam!" Aidan yelled at his bonded dragon. He stood and got in her face.

"I'll get there!" she roared back. She leaned her head backward. Flames shot skyward.

"Hada Spell," Moonbeam said when she calmed down. "Hada. It means fairy in Spanish. The gene of the Fey from another realm long-gone ran through her veins. She left Cliff because she knew the dragon's spirit was with him, but her mind couldn't stand all the feeling of others. She didn't know how to control her ability.

"When she was institutionalized, she met a man, another patient—Matthew O'Rourke, Rennin's grandfather."

Aidan shook his head. "No. He was MIA in Vietnam."

"*MIA*," Moonbeam stressed. "*Missing,* not dead."

Aidan's breath came faster. "Tell me the rest."

"In Vietnam, the dragon's spirit saved him. It became very real. Esmeralda visited him in a POW camp. He escaped. When he told his commanding officers about a florescent green dragon, they committed him without telling his family he lived. He knew too many government secrets to be crazy. He met Hada. They shared something no one else understood. They fell in love and made Cliff."

A sob caught in the great beast's throat. "The government did what they call a lobotomy on Matthew. His essence was gone. Hada. Oh! She suffocated him. She released his spirit. They had let her keep the baby to calm her, but she knew she was next. Cliff had grown up to three in a loony bin. She killed several people to get out. She was on the run until she left Cliff. Cliff is Rennin's uncle. Uncle Cliff for real."

Moonbeam nudged Laurel with her snout. "You know, she'll fight loving you now. She'll say you're related."

"Not close enough to count."

"Do you love her?"

"Yep. I can't explain love at first sight."

"You're destined to be together."

"I know."

Sam rattling the cage got their attention. He pointed at Laurel. "Se-ji."

Aidan stood. "I'll find him." He turned to Moonbeam. "Moonbeam, carry on with the plan. Get them to Miami tonight. Let Uncle Craig know there won't be any from Puma Pass."

"But Laurel."

"I'll take care of her."

As he spoke, Laurel groaned. "Go now!" Aidan said.

Moonbeam pulled the cages to her chest and took wing.

Aidan knelt by Laurel. She bolted up. "Get away!"

"Stop. I know it all. It doesn't change our mission."

14

Ash Snow

"**Those** memories!" Laurel screamed.

"Calm, Sunrise."

"Don't fucking call me that—*cousin*!"

"Not close."

"Did you know?"

"No. Let me explain about the inherited memories." He held up a hand when she started to protest. "All humans have it, but most suppress them. Even those who accept them don't have total recall; thus, déjà vu and things you just think were dreams.

"The first dragon hatchlings on Draconis took a long time to remember all the past. When Quazel killed the ancient beings, much of the link died. Even now, Draco has the most memories because he pieced what Alexander taught him together with the genetic imprints. The dragons have more inherited memory than any other creature.

"Moonbeam didn't mean for all the memories to flow like that. And your memories burst out. She had no control over your memories."

"I saw so much," she said, her voice reticent. "All the way back to Druids. I, not me, but it felt like me, wore a long robe and presided over rituals."

"That explains it. You're from the priesthood, just like my mother."

"There's more. There were magical beings."

"Yes. The faerie realm disappeared before the dragons or mages."

"What am I?"

Aidan chuckled. "My Sunrise."

She sighed.

Aidan whispered, "A lost link, but not if we don't save these people. We still have a mission. We have to find someone named Sergio."

He helped her stand. "Answer one more question," she murmured.

"What?"

"Are there fairies on Draconis?"

"Not that I know of."

He looked east. "Moonbeam is bedding down somewhere in the Ozarks. She'll never make it to Miami before dawn."

He set about making a fire and food. Laurel stared into space, still trying to comprehend all she had seen. Aidan handed her toasted cheese sandwiches and a juice packet. "Eat and let's rest. We'll need to travel some by day. We can't wait for Moonbeam to get back."

Moonbeam nestled the cages into a thick grove of pines. "Sam, is this enough shade for your people?"

Sam nodded.

"Okay. Can you eat raw fish? Or I can cook it."

"Cook." Sam smiled at the dragon, his top teeth only slightly buck.

She grinned back. *He'd be a handsome human without the facial distortions.* "Okay. Let me do this before sunrise."

Moonbeam managed to get at least two trout per person and swallowed a dozen for herself before she plunged beneath the plummeting cascade near the pines. Nothing but her nostrils showed in the churning water.

Mid-morning in Colorado, Aidan handed Laurel a cup of freeze-dried coffee. "Rise and shine. We need to move. I feel an urgency."

"Empathic ability?" She drank a swig. "Ugh! Not the real thing."

He laughed. "I do make good coffee. And, no, not my ability unless folks are nearby."

"You can read me?"

"A little, but you put up walls. Are you still upset?"

She turned the tin cup back and forth between her palms. "Overwhelmed. I never realized all this existed."

"I understand." He handed her fruit and cereal bars. *She's not ready to talk.* "Eat up."

"How are we moving?"

He pointed to packs and rope. "A little mountain climbing."

Not much later, harnessed and ready to repel, Laurel said, "I've never gone down a mountain, only walls in training."

"I've done a little back home. Daddy loves rock climbing. Of course, Moonbeam would have caught me if I'd fallen. Just stay above me."

Aidan pushed off. It took them most of the day to descend. Down, both collapsed against the rock face.

"I don't plan to ever do that again," Laurel panted. "I think I have monster blisters even with gloves."

"Well, we're down, and it looks like a semblance of living within a short walk. Is that a diner?" He pointed to a neon sign in the distance. "I've seen pictures, but never thought I'd see a real one."

"Yep. Looks like something right out of a 1950s movie. Real greasy spoon. Yum."

"You think it's safe?"

"Should be. Another twenty miles west, and we'll run into razor-wire barriers and armed patrols. They won't really be looking for us to sneak *into* the borderlands."

"Borderlands?"

"Yeah. Although there's a good stretch of land that is uncontaminated, the government has put in a barrier almost straight north and south through New Mexico, Colorado, Wyoming, and Montana. Some say it's to protect those of us out here—others believe it's to give the people who were infected some space to heal. Still, there are those who think it's just a buffer zone and anyone stupid enough to go in deserves whatever happens, and any of the others who try to come out are just walking target practice."

"What do you think?"

"I think there's some truth to all of it and some serious lies besides."

"Yeah. You're probably right. Well, let's take advantage of the food and move out. We'll deal with whatever comes our way."

She felt her pockets. "Yes, I have the cash Grandpa gave me. We have to pay to eat in a diner."

They shouldered their packs and trudged to the establishment down the road. Inside greeted them with uniformed guards carrying automatic weapons.

"Shit," muttered Laurel.

"Sh. There are a few civilians."

"Yeah, but this is a bad-boy hangout."

"Do we look like backpackers?"

"Doesn't matter. Not much of that going on these days out here."

"Sit where you can find a place," called out a pot-bellied man with a full beard and bald head.

Trying to avoid contact with any of the perimeter guards, Aidan and Laurel moved to a booth for two near the back closest to the kitchen. They dropped their packs against the wall and sat down. Plexiglas covered menus on the tables. After Aidan's stomach trumpeted his hunger, a woman who must have been the bald man's wife came over.

"What can I get you?" she wheezed, short of breath.

"Laurel?" Aidan deferred to her to order first.

"What a handsome gentleman," said the waitress.

"Yes, ma'am," Laurel said. "I'll have the bacon cheeseburger, fully dressed, extra onions." She grinned. "Chili cheese fries and a large fruit salad. Coke."

"You must be starving."

"Mountain climbing."

"Good to see some normal life." She turned to Aidan. "For you, hon?"

"The large bacon cheeseburger with everything—cheddar cheese and add jalapenos. Bacon cheese fries with ranch dipping sauce and an order of onion rings with comeback sauce. Vanilla Coke."

"Coming right up." She waddled away.

"I wonder how many little dolls she has under that apron," Laurel said with a giggle.

"What?"

"She's built like a matryoshka doll."

"A what?" Aidan tilted his head.

"A Russian doll made of wood. Inside are a lot of smaller dolls. You go from big to small, sometimes six or seven dolls."

"That's mean. She was nice."

"Yeah. I guess. But she thought you were handsome, and I was starving." She laughed out loud. "Do you have any idea what you ordered?"

"Not really, but it sounded good."

When the woman brought their order, she brought a little side table to hold everything. As they ate, a guard approached.

"You're not from around here," he said, his weapon across his forearm.

"No," Aidan said, detecting great hostility from the soldier. "We're from Miami."

"You do have a good tan." He pointed at Laurel. "But she looks like a porcelain doll."

Aidan sensed a wave of rage washing over Laurel. He took her hand across the table. "Not everyone from Miami lives on the beach. Where are you from?" Aidan tried friendliness to defuse the situation.

"Vermont." The guard's eyes raked over Laurel.

Aidan began to feel his own rush of ire.

Laurel reached into her backpack, retrieved her dog tags and captain's bars, and slammed them onto the table. "Corporal!" she snapped. "Do you recognize these items?"

"Yeah. They would indicate a Navy flier, rank of captain. Where'd you come by them?"

She stood and jammed her finger into the guard's chest. "Captain Laurel Elaine Moss, United States Navy. On special assignment. If you don't salute me within the next fifteen seconds, I'm going to have your ass court martialed, you pompous, disrespectful shit."

The corporal stepped back. Eying his superior officer, he realized she was not joking. He saluted sharply.

"At ease," she said after returning the salute. She sat back down and pointed to her companion. "Aidan O'Rourke, foreign diplomat. Corporal, we're on special assignment. We need entrance into the restricted area."

"Just the two of you? Unarmed?"

"We have weapons," Aidan said, pointing at the sub-machine gun. "Just a different kind."

"You want me to let you through, Captain?"

"Yes, Corporal?" She widened her eyes in question.

"Montjoy. Bentley Montjoy."

Laurel blinked and shook her head slightly. *Definitely pompous.* "Yes, Corporal Montjoy, we need your help."

"Well, might I suggest you go in the morning? The borderlands are often swarmed at night."

"How do you discourage them?" Aidan asked, feeling a tightening in his chest.

"Just shoot the suckers. Keep the buzzards happy."

Aidan clenched the napkin he held so tightly his knuckles turned white.

"Not anymore," Laurel said sternly. "Fire over their heads. No more killing. What if you've jeopardized our mission?"

"Your mission?"

"We've been sent to find one person."

"Person?"

"Yes, Corporal. They are *people*. For our own safety, we'll go in the morning, but there will be no more killing. Who's your commander?"

"Right now, it's Lieutenant Ralston."

"I'll speak to him with these orders. Now, we'd like to finish our meal and find a place to sleep."

Montjoy stood rooted as the waitress came back. She said, "I overheard. We got a room you can have tonight."

Laurel glowered at the corporal. "Dismissed, Montjoy."

Montjoy moved to a group coming in. The waitress leaned closer. "You just made an enemy, honey. I'm Tilba Cruz. Who are you looking for?"

"Man named Sergio," Aidan said, feeling a cooperative spirit.

"Hm. Doctor Sergio, I bet. Head up San Francisco way."

A tall black man with lieutenant stripes approached the table. "Lieutenant Arjun Ralston." He saluted Laurel.

She nodded. "Pull up a chair."

He sat down and Laurel explained only that they needed to get through to the restricted area immediately.

"So, you don't want to wait for morning?" asked Ralston.

"Time is of the essence," Aidan replied.

"I can let you through, but then you're on your own." He handed both of them a nine-millimeter handgun. "I understand we're not to shoot to kill."

"That's right," said Laurel.

"You won't mind if I check into this?"

"Go ahead. Call the Pentagon and ask for Admiral Sylvester Bolton, and then locate Lieutenant Colonel Clifton Spell."

Ralston glared at her. *She's either a great liar, or this is for real.* "Yes, ma'am. I don't think the admiral will be in this time of night. You're in Mountain Time. That would be Eastern."

Tilba came up with a packed box of food. She noticed Aidan and Laurel had eaten every bite they ordered. "Your to-go order." She grinned.

Ralston stood. "You ready then, Captain?" Ralston headed toward the door.

Laurel reached for the money to pay their tab. Tilba touched her hand. "Already taken care of." She leaned close to Aidan's ear. "Dr. Sergio Muñoz is my nephew."

"Muñoz?"

She nodded. "We've heard rumors here that some mutants near San Francisco aren't all gone nuts, you know. Stories spread about a doctor searching for a cure though he's infected himself. My nephew chose to stay behind after the first attack, risking infection. He *would* stay and help. That's the kind of person he is. When you get through the fence, walk a mile down the highway. You'll find lots of cars for the taking."

Laurel and Aidan stood. Laurel took Tilba's hand. "Thank you."

Tilba held on to Laurel's hand, rolled her eyes and tipped her head toward the entrance. "Don't trust a one of them, except maybe Arjun."

Laurel cocked an eyebrow.

"He's okay," Tilba continued. "Just angry. The rest"—She rolled her eyes again—"They'll shoot you in the back and leave you for the vultures. I'm calling the Pentagon myself and asking for that admiral. I'll tell him where you've gone."

The two outsiders followed Ralston down the road to an electrified gate. The trek took quite some time.

"Couldn't you get a jeep?" Laurel asked.

"Could've, but I thought the walk might make you wait until daylight." He signaled the guard manning it to open.

With a look of confusion, the man obeyed. Laurel and Aidan went through and heard the click and buzz.

"Don't look back," Aidan whispered.

"Why?"

"He's pointing his gun at us. He wants to shoot us."

"Your empathic ability?"

"Yep. He feels you upstaged him, and he resents it, but there's something else. He's afraid we'll hurt somebody out here—a loved one that's infected. That's why he's angry and why he requested this assignment."

"He's a bad person. Moonbeam can eat him."

"He's not bad, but he'd make her sick. He's like a red-hot chili pepper on steroids. He's near his exploding point."

They kept walking into the gathering darkness. A mile up the road, they found dozens of abandoned cars just as Tilba had said.

Laurel pointed to a yellow Hummer. "I've always wanted one of these."

"I guess it's as good as any." Aidan looked toward her. "You'll have to operate it. I have no idea how to use one."

They climbed into the vehicle. Laurel hesitated to try and crank it. "You know, until we get to San Francisco, it might be wise to travel during the day since these bio-chem mutants will be out at night. Once there, we'll have to use disguises."

With the food for the trip in the back of the car, Aidan said, "Good idea. Will it be okay to sleep in this thing?"

"This *thing* is a Hummer. Yeah, I think it will be." She crawled into the backseat, found a release to lower the back of the seat, and waved her hand. "Instant bed."

Aidan unfurled his sleeping bag. "Instant blanket." He grinned.

She gave him the come-hither finger. He went to her. "Instant teddy bear," she teased. "We need to hide now. I see movement."

Moonbeam set down in the parking lot of the overlook by The Everglades. Margaret, Randall, and Marshall waited. They immediately rushed forward with bags of burgers.

Moonbeam said, "Sam, they have food."

Sam grunted and made motions to the other quasi-captives. They accepted the nourishment with surprising calm.

Margaret said, "I have food for you too, Moonbeam." She presented the dragon with a tub of assorted fowl.

Char popped up from the marsh.

"Grandfather!" Moonbeam squealed, happy to see him. They shared the standard dragon greeting, touching both cheeks.

Char grinned when the younger dragon slid her tub toward him to share. "I ate already, dear one." He nuzzled her cheek but jerked back as the memories from her mental sharing with Laurel went straight to him.

"What the?" he asked, his heart rate increasing.

"You'll share with Cliff?"

"Of course, I will."

Randall and Marshall brought over boxes of sleep pants and t-shirts.

"Sam," Margaret said. "I'm Margaret, Laurel's grandmother."

"Lo-lo groan-mare?" He looked confused, and then seemed enlightened. "Ah!" He touched Mary's abdomen. "Lo-lo." Then he pointed at Margaret. "Magee." Then he pointed away.

"I think you got it," Margaret said with a smile. She lifted some of the clothes from the box. "Clothes." She ran her hand down her body. "To cover."

"Ugh!" Preceded a long sigh. "Ow." He patted different areas of his body.

"Clothes hurt your skin?"

He nodded.

"These are very soft," Randall said. "Craig sent word that some cloth hurt the people he's already working with."

He handed a pair of soft flannel pants to Sam. "Try it."

Sam took the garment and Randall mimed putting them on. Sam hesitated, but finally put on the pajama pants.

"Okay?" Randall asked.

Sam nodded. "Oo-k."

In short time all the confined folks were covered. Some whimpered. Margaret took a moment to check them. "It seems these three still hurt. Where?"

Sam gestured and made sounds. All three touched the elastic waist bands.

Margaret nodded. "Thought that might be an issue." She got three pairs of draw-string pants and handed them to the three. "Change."

When they had changed pants, Margaret tied the pants loosely. "Better?"

They made noises. Sam said, "Oo-k."

"We need to go," Char intoned. "I only have about six hours before dawn. I'll have to hide in the Rain Forest and continue tomorrow."

"And I need to get back to the Ozarks and then to Aidan," Moonbeam added. "I have a funny feeling about him."

"You think that boy has done something crazy, like the first Rennin when he jumped from the cliff to see if I was fast enough to catch him?"

She nodded. Char closed his eyes and sent the fear to Smoke to relay to Rennin.

The dragons participated in their dragon hug. Moonbeam called, "Good luck!" and flew west.

Char gathered the cages and winged south.

All night, Aidan and Laurel heard screeching and grunting. Sleep came intermittently. Apparently, the infected beings were hunting, feeding, and breeding.

Laurel groaned and buried her head against Aidan's chest.

He chuckled. "We could do the same thing, and our noises would go unnoticed."

She bit him on his left rib cage.

"Damn it! That hurt!" he snapped.

"And just how many times have you enjoyed such frivolity and noisemaking?"

"None. Go to sleep." He turned away from her.

"Sorry. The Prince of the Isle never has? Wow!" She spooned against him, draping her arm over him. He took her hand and pulled it to his lips.

"Me neither," she said, and put her cheek against his bare back.

They awoke at dawn, stiff-necked and achy.

Aidan opened the food Tilba had sent. "Pastries and juice," he said.

Laurel nodded. "Wrapped securely so they can't be smelled. Señora Cruz knows stuff."

They ate and then Laurel tried to start the car whose key dangled in the ignition. "Damn it!" She hit the steering wheel with the heel of her hand. "They've been idle so long the batteries are dead."

"All of them?"

"I don't know. We'll have to try others."

"Sorry. I know you wanted this one."

"It doesn't matter. We'll have to go on foot in the end and with contact lenses."

"When this is all over, I'll get you one of these."

"What use would I have for this on Draconis?"

Aidan smiled and made no comment. Laurel had not caught her own slip of the tongue.

Finally finding an old PT Cruiser with a full tank of gas and a charged battery, sailor and spy drove toward the Bay Area.

The farther northeast they traveled, the colder it became, even colder than Pikes Peak.

Closer and closer to their destination, Aidan stared out the window. "Laurel, what is that on the side of the road? It looks like snow drifts, but it's gray."

She stopped the car and used the Geiger counter. "Ash snow. It's left over from the radiation fallout."

Aidan put the meter out the window. The clicks were low and slow.

Laurel nodded. "Some radiation, but not dangerous, but we'll want to get in and out."

She started driving. "We're thirty miles from where you think we should go. We'll need to stay hidden and observe for a day or two."

"So, is it time to go on foot?"

"At dark. Let's eat and get ready. I'll drive us as close as possible."

15
B·A·M·F·

As Laurel continued to drive along, a loud thump, a sputter, and smoke from under the hood signaled the end of one car.

"Well, shit!" she exclaimed. "And we are so close. I guess we hike or find another car."

"Well, there seems to be no shortage of abandoned cars if they'll—crank. That's the right word?"

"Yeah, Island Boy, it is." She began to gather her pack. "Let's see if we get lucky."

I wish I could "get lucky." Aidan sighed and followed her example.

Walking kept them warm, but the air bit their cheeks. A mile up the road and three unsuccessful tries to start different vehicles, strange movement caught Aidan's eye.

"Laurel!" he whispered urgently. "I thought bio-chem victims didn't travel by day."

"They don't. Why?"

He caught her arm. "Someone or *something* is out there stalking us."

"Could it be a cougar or a bear?"

"It's dogging our steps too closely to be an animal."

"You think functional bio-chem victim like Sam?"

He shrugged. "I'm sensing anger and hostility. I have a bad feeling."

With wild war whoops, half a dozen humans, not affected by bio-chem, leapt over cars and from behind boulders toward the duo.

Laurel and Aidan stood back-to-back.

"Who are you and what do you want?" the Navy flier demanded with an air of authority. "You aren't even supposed to be here."

"Well, we're here, little lady," growled a scraggly, greasy-haired, snaggle-toothed man. "We want whatever you got, and maybe you."

"Like hell," said Aidan, letting his backpack slide to the ground and dropping into a front stance. "Captain Moss, you *are* trained in hand-to-hand, I suppose."

"Naturally." She let her pack hit the ground.

Aidan kicked himself mentally for not having put weapons of some sort on a belt. The would-be gang circled the two weaponless pilgrims, knives and the guns Ralston had given them being inside their packs. Armed with clubs and knives, they attacked by swarm.

Laurel's foot caught the crotch of one attacker with a shaved head before she realized it was a woman, and her defensive strike did very little damage. She blocked a downward smack from a club.

"Solar plexus, Sunrise!" Aidan yelled over his shoulder as his foot landed against the jaw of the snaggle-puss leader. "That'll put the bitch on the ground, sucking wind."

Another assailant swung hard with a long stick toward Aidan. He ducked and the weapon whacked into Snaggle-Puss, leaving him out cold. A switchblade clattered from his hand.

Laurel caught Big-boned Woman with a palm-heel strike to the solar plexus as Aidan had suggested. The large woman crumpled, gasping to breathe. Laurel finished her with a vicious kick to the chin.

Aidan swung around and grappled the pole from his second foe. He instantly turned it into a bo and masterfully rendered its original wielder unconscious. He instructed Laurel, "Get the woman's club and another. Use them like tonfas. Kick some ass, Sunrise."

Meanwhile, Laurel snatched the broken baseball bat the female had held and went after a slow-moving man twice her size. This time her well-aimed foot connected and brought the monster of a man to his knees. Without hesitation, she walloped him upside the head with her confiscated weapon and took the club he had.

Laurel gave chase to a scrawny, emaciated man who turned tail and ran.

Several more gang members emerged from behind abandoned cars. Aidan swung his improvised bo with skill and strength. He pounced onto the roof of a car with cat-like agility. Alternately, he swung the bo and placed strategic kicks.

After more than half an hour, ten people lay either unconscious or groaning in pain from bruised, battered, and broken body parts.

Holding the bo in both hands, Aidan jumped to the ground. He leaned with clenched fists on both knees, catching his own breath in heaves.

Laurel ran up with blood-covered batons. Aidan raised the bo to strike whoever was approaching. Laurel blocked the staff with her short club. "Whoa! It's me, Jackie Chan."

She looked around her and pointed the way she had come. "Three more that way. Wow! I had no idea you were such a *bamf*!"

"A what?"

"Bad-ass motherfucker."

"I *think* that's a compliment. Not bad yourself, Fireball." He managed a chuckle. "But, um, did your grandmother ever wash your mouth out with soap?"

She gusted a long breath and found water in their packs, passing some to Aidan.

Both drank extended draughts. Laurel laughed outright. "Nope. Soap probably wouldn't have worked on me anyway." She pointed around. "Must be some folks who didn't make it out. No way will the military let them through now. They've ganged for survival."

"Looters. Predators," Aidan argued.

Laurel laughed. "Looks like they took on the wrong prey. Let's find a car and get where we need to go."

They picked up their packs. "Before we go, let's put our own weapons in our belts. We might find more of these cutthroats," Aidan suggested.

They improvised a sheath for a knife and a holster for the nine-millimeter and left the thugs where they lay. A few miles farther, Laurel found another car that started. They drove to the beach.

Part Three

Define Captive

16

Infiltration

As the sun slid into the Pacific Ocean, Aidan and Laurel watched the sunset through strangely clouded eyes.

"Whoever made these did a good job," Laurel stated. "I can see just fine."

"But you look funny."

"Ha, ha." She pulled him into an old Snack Shack on Fisherman's Wharf. "Hidden, remember? Sam's not here to help." She pointed through the plate glass window. "You didn't sense anything, did you?"

Aidan saw the first human stirring. "No. It feels like a damper of some sort. I'm not even sensing you." He scowled. "I feel kind of...empty."

"Could be the residual radiation."

"I don't need my gift to tell me these people are different. That one is wearing clothes."

"Thank God! I thought we would need to run around naked." She pushed her unruly hair back and sat behind cracked blinds to watch as more beings congregated.

"I might have enjoyed the view." Aidan sat across from her with a grin on his face.

"You don't give up."

"Nope. Looks as if they're going fishing. Providing for the collective."

"Cooperative rule?"

He replied, "That woman seems to be giving orders and not in grunts and gestures."

"I see. We aren't dealing with inferior creatures."

She sat back, but only for a second. "Oh, shit!"

"Oh, shit!" Aidan echoed.

"That woman noticed the car. We really have to hide." She dragged Aidan into the walk-in cooler.

Moonbeam landed in the camp. She spun around in circles. "Where are you? No, no!" She sniffed the air and found the rappel rope. "Aidan Alexander O'Rourke! You did this on purpose."

She sent the information to both Smoke and Char. Both sent the same instructions. "Trail them, but stay hidden. A lady named Tilba Cruz called Admiral Bolton. She said they were headed toward San Francisco."

After a group of mutants walked through the Snack Shack, Laurel and Aidan emerged from their hiding place.

"Well, they *are* organized," Laurel muttered as she sank back into the chair she had occupied before.

"I guess we had better go on to Puma Pass. Sergio Muñoz. He has to be related to Daddy's old friend. There was a hospital in Puma Pass. He might be using it for his research."

"Good thinking." She returned to the freezer and came out with frozen pizza.

"What's that?" Aidan asked.

"Food."

"Is it contaminated?"

Laurel held the Geiger counter against it. "Nope and not expired either." She turned on a toaster oven. "Yes! It works."

A short time later, she set three pizzas on the table. They ate in silence.

Finally, Laurel said, "In the morning we'll drive to Puma Pass, find a place to hide the car, and hike in. We'll blend in and try to find this Sergio."

Aidan made up a sleeping area behind the counter in case someone looked in. Laurel touched his shoulder. "Why so quiet?"

"I'm not sensing *anything*. It makes me feel empty and scared. I never realized how much sensing emotion in my environment meant to me." He rubbed his hands down his face.

"Hey! I'm sure it's just the radiation. Or it could be they don't have any."

"Sam did. *You* do."

"It's okay." She hugged him.

Aidan breathed in relief. *I don't have to be empathic to feel you care.*

Next morning, they found more food from the freezer, used the facilities to clean up and change clothes, and drove to Puma Pass.

The roads were nearly impassable, forcing them to hike sooner than intended. Laurel put the car in a packed parking lot of abandoned vehicles.

"It's really cold," Aidan said as they walked.

"Yeah." She pointed. "There's Mercier Memorial Hospital. Want to check it out? The town is that way, and the mines are just out from the town, according to the maps."

"Yeah, let's look."

Opening the door to the ER entrance to the hospital, both stopped in their tracks. A number of cloudy-eyed people appeared to be working in the facility.

They ducked out. "These people are totally normal except for a few cosmetic things," Aidan gasped.

"At least they appear to be, but they are staying out of the sun."

"Just where we should go."

"Yeah."

They walked briskly back to the parking area. "What now, Captain?" Aidan asked.

"Let's go to the mines, hide nearby, and join the herd when they come out."

They hiked for hours. Only the sun warmed them as they neared Puma Pass. Aidan stopped. "That house." He pointed and walked to a huge early-Victorian-style house. "This is where my parents lived before Daddy was taken and buried alive. Then they moved to Mom's Trading Post."

Aidan walked onto the porch of the old house. Turning the doorknob, showed it unlocked. The two of them stepped inside the dark dwelling.

"Do you sense anything?" Laurel asked.

"Love, violence, more love, but from bygone days. Nobody's here. We'll be safe inside."

They dropped their supplies near the door, found the sofa, and collapsed into an exhausted sleep.

They jumped awake as something bumped the door. Looking through a window, Aidan said, "It's that woman."

"You sure it's the same person?"

"Yes. She's coming here."

They shoved their belongings in the under-the-stairs closet and made their way through the house and out the back door.

A few of the residents had begun to stir in the late afternoon light, but they still kept to shadow.

Laurel and Aidan crept back to the front of the house. The woman entered the house. Ducking below a windowsill, Aidan and Laurel strained to hear.

The woman stopped and appeared to sniff the air. Then she gave hand signals to several of the others.

Before either knew what was happening, Laurel and Aidan were surrounded. Several people dragged them back into the house and shoved them to their knees before the woman.

She lifted both their chins with an index finger. "You smell like sunlight," she said in a husky voice. "Your disguises are believable." She smiled. "Who are you and what are you up to?"

Aidan shivered. Anger rolled from this woman. Laurel clutched his hand, feeling his fear.

"I'll try to make this easy," the woman said. "I'm Nidia Muñoz…"

"Muñoz?" Aidan blurted. "We're looking for Sergio Muñoz. Sam sent us. And Tilba Cruz."

"Very likely. Who are you?"

"I'm Aidan O'Rourke. I've come to help. This is Laurel Moss."

"Huh-huh." She signaled, and a number of others went to bind Aidan's and Laurel's hands.

"Sergio isn't here right now. We'll just keep you around until he comes. Maybe we'll have a few conversations."

A shimmer enveloped Aidan. Suddenly, a white wolf sat beside Laurel. Aidan's voice said, "Change to your spirit guide."

"How?" she screamed.

The wolf bared his fangs and leapt toward Nidia. Before he reached her, a blunt object bashed his head.

A crowd surrounded Aidan and Laurel as they were dragged through the town to the old gold mines. Aidan jerked his hands. They were bound. He brushed them across his face and felt sticky ooze. *Blood.*

They were lowered into a deep pit, part of an abandoned mine.

"Where Rennin and Bart Mercier were forced to mine gold," Aidan mumbled. "I can still feel the evil and the good."

"Your inherited memories?" Laurel whispered.

"Yes."

Silence screamed above them as all the people left.

"What happened back there?" Laurel asked, her tied hands brushing Aidan's long blond hair away from a gash of drying blood as he lay motionless on the ground.

"Spirit guide manifested. I didn't control it well."

"Yours is a wolf?"

"Yes. Yours?"

"Albatross. I didn't know how to manifest, or I could have flown away. Too late now. We're tied up."

"It's okay. We'll get out of here."

"You might," Nidia said above them. "We'll talk. You are something I've never seen. We'll see if you can help."

"I have to speak to Sergio," Aidan demanded.

"You are not going anywhere near my brother."

17

Cities of Refuge

"**We** can help!" Aidan yelled at the retreating figure.

Nidia came back. "I doubt it. The government sent you—special assignment. Help? More likely, you're here to sabotage Sergio's work. Two years ago, we were just like the others. All of us here have submitted to trial treatments. So, what if we die?" She shrugged. "As you can see, we've progressed."

"Sergio sounds brilliant. If I could just talk to him, I'm sure Uncle Craig, who's a doctor also, could team up and find the cure."

"Have to find the cause first." Nidia laughed, hard and cold.

"Uncle Craig can help."

Their captor snorted. "We had an outside doctor come in. He was too afraid of us to function. Thought we were cannibals."

She put her hand on top of her head, her cloudy eyes momentarily flashing black. "Want to see something?"

"Sure."

She lifted a long, straight, black wig from her head to reveal a bald scalp covered in oozing and scabbed sores.

Laurel gasped. Aidan gagged.

"Courtesy of the outside help," Nidia said. "You see, I can go into the sun if I'm covered. The baldness is from radiation poisoning. The unhealing lesions came when the good doctor pushed me out the hospital door. Sergio dragged him to the barrier. The guards shot him, grazed his shoulder, but he left that whimpering worm and came back to work on an antidote. He discovered several of his experiments had been destroyed."

She arranged her wig back on her head. "Puma Pass is one of a dozen cities of refuge—guaranteed safety."

"How did you know to look for us?" Laurel asked.

A mirthless laugh escaped Nidia's lips. "The phones work. Lieutenant Ralston called me, Captain Moss."

"You have to listen," Laurel pled.

"Nope." With that, she left them alone at the bottom of the shaft.

Aidan called after Nidia, "You're not safe here! There are no cities of refuge. You're a target."

His words fell on deaf ears.

Lieutenant Colonel Clifton Spell and Rennin O'Rourke sat in an office with Admiral Sylvester Bolton. A map lay open on a round table.

Bolton pointed to a number of highlighted areas worldwide. "These, gentlemen, are cities of refuge, places for infected people to live in safety."

"Bullshit!" Cliff Spell snapped. He noted two in South America. "These two, I know for a fact, are concentration camps."

"How do you know?"

"I did some recon."

"They can only be seen from the air."

"Private, top secret transportation."

Frustration filling his voice, Bolton said, "Cliff, I'm trying to help."

"I know that, and eventually I'll tell you all."

Rennin touched several other areas. He noted three on the United States' West Coast, two in Eastern Europe, one in Alaska, one in Siberia, and three very close to North Korea. He pointed out only one in Africa and Australia's lack of any. He scratched his chin.

"Admiral, were these people told these were places of safety?"

"Yes, Rennin, they were."

"And they believed it. They functioned well enough to get to one in most cases. This is no more than herding them into a slaughterhouse. What happened to the United States battling for human rights? This is genocide. All these governments are in agreement—first time, and it's for evil." He straightened up. "We have to stop it. There's no way we can get all these people out in time."

Cliff added, "According to Ming and Zane, troops are rounding up strays and taking them to these camps. The only cities of refuge that don't resemble concentration camps are on The U.S. West Coast.

Stragglers continue to arrive at them though, and they have no way to escape. The barrier fence runs from the Mexican border to the Canadian border. And those two countries have erected barricades to keep any of our folks out. That gives new meaning to border patrol. Finally, they're cut off by the Pacific Ocean."

Cliff circled Alcatraz. "Is this part of the Bay Area refuge?"

"No," Bolton replied. "It's deserted."

"Are you sure?"

"Why?" The admiral sat back and glared at his old friend.

"I saw people there."

"Mutants?"

"Yep, but very organized and operating boats."

"I have to tell the Joint Chiefs."

"No," Cliff said with authority. "If you do, they'll just target it." He turned to Rennin. "We should make that our base of operations, and I'd put money on Laurel and Aidan having learned something that's sent them that direction."

"Makes sense. That's why the woman called the admiral." Rennin agreed.

"How are you going to get there?" Bolton demanded. "I want to know, and now."

Rennin and Cliff exchanged looks. Rennin nodded. Cliff said, "Sit back, Sly. You're not going to believe this."

Laurel and Aidan slept. Rattling noises above them startled them awake. Metal buckets with food and water were being lowered.

Aidan caught the sustenance and called to the person serving them, "Hello. What's your name?"

A preteen girl peered into the pit. "Hope."

"I'm Aidan and this is Laurel." He placed a hand on her shoulder. "Hope, do you know where Sergio is? We must speak to him."

"I'm not supposed to talk to you. Mom will be angry."

"Is Nidia your mother?" *I'm getting a little sensitivity back.*

"Yes. My father died."

"I'm sorry," Laurel said. "Both my parents died when I was just a baby. I know how you feel."

Hope looked over her shoulder. "Mom's coming. Don't tell I talked to you."

"Okay," they said together.

"Hope, what are you doing?" Nidia asked.

"You told me to feed them."

"So, I did. Go on now.

"Nidia," Aidan called. "Please listen to what we have to say."

"What could be so important?"

"You're going to die—all of you if you don't listen."

"Dragons?" It must have been the twentieth time Bolton had said that one word.

"Yes," Rennin and Cliff said in unison, annoyance edging their voices.

Bolton stood. "Prove it."

"Okay," Rennin said. "Do you prefer Pennsylvania or Florida?"

"How many are here?"

"Let's see," Rennin said. "Moonbeam is out West looking for Aidan and Laurel. She will *not* hesitate to incinerate anything or anyone who threatens my son. Smoke, my bonded dragon…"

"Bonded?" Bolton interrupted.

"We have an emotional and mental link. Smoke is in Mom's Trading Post, Pennsylvania, waiting for us to get back. Char, who's bonded to Cliff, is in Miami, and Scarlet, Esmeralda, and Filigree are in the Himalayas. Smoke and Char are son and father. They're the ones who came here years ago when Continental Flight 777 went down over the Atlantic. The pilot wasn't crazy. They came to take my family, so I'd go to Draconis. We can have a squadron of two dozen here in thirty-six hours."

"Okay," said Bolton. "Show me Smoke. He's the closest."

A few hours later, the three men stepped from the car at Rennin's home on Beaver Creek. Rennin called, "Smoke!"

The gargantuan gray dragon lifted from the water.

"Oh, my God!" Bolton stammered.

Cliff placed a hand on his old friend's shoulder. "If you want to protect the cities of refuge, you just met your Celtic guardian."

18
Rubbing Salt in the Wound

Admiral Bolton entered a meeting of military and international leaders at the Pentagon with Rennin O'Rourke and Clifton Spell flanking him.

"What's the meaning of this intrusion?" demanded the Vice President of the United States, sitting at the head of the table and the apparent chairman of the group.

Standing straight and tall, green eyes flashing authority, Rennin said, "We're here to stop you from committing genocide."

"Who are you?" asked a Korean in heavy-accented English.

"I am Rennin Duncan O'Rourke formerly known as Troy Lane Tomerson."

A few gasps showed name recognition.

Rennin indicated his comrades with a head tilt to each. "Admiral Sylvester Bolton and Lieutenant Colonel Clifton Spell. You must be Kim Hajoon. Does your father know you're here?"

The young Korean tapped the side of his head to show he felt his father was insane. "My father."

"Perhaps." Rennin's voice showed sarcasm.

"You have no business here," Vice President Carson Geoghegan (Go-HAY-gan) said. "How did you get past the sentries?"

Rennin waved a hand. "That's not important."

"I beg to differ," said Geoghegan.

"Shit," muttered Rennin to his companions. "Very strong-minded." To those gathered he said, "The guards will not be bothering us." He stared Geoghegan down. "Mr. Vice President, does your boss know what's going on? I have it on good authority that President Barbour might be incapacitated."

"Nonsense!" Geoghegan answered, his glare at the intruders threatening. "He's been a bit under the weather."

"Huh-huh. And has he, perchance, gone West for his health problems?"

Geoghegan started to rise. Cliff and Bolton pushed him back into his chair, each with a hand on the man's shoulders.

Rennin looked around at the group. "It would seem that the President of the United States has been infected. I'm certain the Vice President has been waiting for the proper time to take over the Oval Office. I hope we can keep that from happening. We must convince you of the wrongness to kill *all* those affected after your attacks."

Hope's voice called into the darkened colliery, "Aidan, Laurel, I brought more food."

"I can't see you," Aidan said.

"Oh, I forgot your eyes can't penetrate the darkness."

A scratching noise preceded the flicker of light as the child lit a lantern. She set it on the edge of the pit and lowered two buckets, one filled with very salty smoked herring, boiled potatoes, crisp raw carrots and sourdough bread and the other with fresh water.

"Thanks," Aidan said.

"You're welcome. Mom has gone to see Uncle Sergio. What did you mean you came to help and we're all going to die?" She sat with her feet dangling over the side of the opening.

The captives ate what was offered to them. Around a mouthful, Aidan said, "We have good reason to believe that world governments are meeting and planning to use something called napalm to burn all the cities of refuge."

"B-b-but," the little girl stammered, "they said we'd be safer here. Are you sure?"

"Yes, Hope," Laurel said, her tone one of compassion.

"They lied?" Tears choked Hope's voice. "It's their fault we're all like this. They told Uncle Sergio to keep researching, and they'd give him whatever supplies he needed. They do food drops every week."

"Jeez!" Laurel snapped. "It'll be so easy. These people won't suspect a thing. They'll think they're getting a supply drop."

"What can we do?" asked Hope.

"Get your mom to listen to us," Aidan said.

"I'll try." She left, taking the lantern.

"I hate this darkness," Laurel whined.

"It's okay. If we can't get Nidia to listen, at least we'll be safe from the napalm." He chuckled.

"Thanks for trying to cheer me up." She sighed. "I really want to help that little girl."

"Me too." He fumbled in the dark with hands still bound with plastic ties in front to find Laurel's similarly tied hands. "You're freezing."

"It's so cold."

He looped his arms over her and pulled her close. "Relax. By now, Moonbeam's sniffing us out."

"Literally." Laurel laughed lightly and laid her cheek against Aidan's chest. "I sure hope she hurries."

The meeting in Virginia spiraled into a shouting match. "You are accusing me of murder!" yelled Geoghegan.

"Of more than one!" affirmed Rennin.

The Israeli representative stood and pounded the table. "We must listen to these men. My people have been the target of mass extermination too many times for me to sit quietly and let this happen if there is any alternative."

The Russian diplomat countered, "There's nothing to do to help them."

"Not true!" bellowed Rennin. "My son found some who spoke and has gone in search of a doctor who's trying to develop an antidote. The young man, Sam, communicated and tried to protect his pregnant mate. That is *not* the actions of a dumb animal."

Geoghegan squirmed. Rennin pointed a finger at the United States' Vice President. "You know I'm right. You're just rubbing salt in the wound."

Kim stood. "Mr. Vice President, is all Mr. O'Rourke says true? Do you know of this doctor? Is there hope to reverse what my father began?"

The Vice President took a deep breath. "He's vanished. Probably dead."

"Where is he?" Rennin demanded.

"Dr. Sergio Muñoz was in Puma Pass, California."

"Sergio Muñoz!" Rennin leapt across the table and belted Vice President Geoghegan in the mouth.

"You've been talking to my daughter. I don't appreciate that," Nidia screamed into the pit.

Aidan and Laurel jumped awake.

Nidia continued, "You have her terrified of being burned alive."

"Listen to her, please!" Aidan hollered into the darkness.

"Why would our leaders do that?"

"You really have to ask?" Laurel said. "You already said someone sabotaged your brother's work. This is not a city of refuge. It's a death camp."

"That can't be."

Aidan encouraged, "Call Ralston. See what he knows."

"He would let me know."

"You sure?"

"Yes!"

"Why?"

Nidia hissed, "He's Hope's father."

"I thought he died," Laurel said.

"Better she believe that than to know he can never be with us. He was called to active duty just days after she was born. We weren't married, but he does what he can to help us."

"Did he tell you the government plans to incinerate you?" Laurel snapped.

"It can't be true! He would tell me."

"If *he* knows," Laurel cried.

"Call him," Aidan said.

Nidia stormed away. Aidan and Laurel strained their ears to hear snippets of the conversation beyond the cave entrance.

"Is it true?" They heard Nidia scream. "That would be rubbing salt in our already open, bleeding wounds…Find out, damn it!"

Nidia returned to the abandoned gold mine shaft. "You will have no further contact with my daughter. I'll personally see to your needs. If I find out you're lying, I'll kill you. If you're telling the truth, *you* will be my bargaining chips."

She walked away. No amount of entreaty fazed her.

19

Political Prisoners

"*Prizers?*" Sam asked as Dr. Craig Jamison drew blood from his arm through bars on a containment cell. He gazed toward his mate who lay on a cot in the same cell.

"No," Craig said. "You are *not* a prisoner." He sealed the test tube.

Sam placed his hands on the bars. "Cazh amuls." He pointed toward some test subjects who paced and growled without discernible words. He shook his head. "No like. Ay-in hep."

Suddenly, Mary let out a high-pitched scream.

"Ma-ri!" Sam ran back to her, his eyes wide with fear.

Craig opened the cell and went in. He took the young woman's hand and felt her abdomen. "It's okay. You're about to have a baby."

Craig lifted her from her fetal position. "Come on, Sam."

Sam followed, looking at his hands and back at the cage.

"You are *not* a prisoner, Sam. I'm not going to restrain you. Your door was never locked."

Craig stopped by a pretty blonde. "Caitlin, get that vial of blood to d'Aubigné. I want to see if Sam's blood has those same weird-shaped cells as theirs." He dipped his head toward the less civilized people who had come from the Far East. "I have a strange feeling something otherworldly is in play here, but right now I have a baby to deliver."

Seven hours later, loud crying gave proof of healthy lungs. "It's a boy!" Craig announced. He handed the baby to his wife, Casey, who always assisted with births.

Casey cleaned the baby off and weighed him. "Seven pounds, two ounces," she informed. "Not bad." She gave the baby to his father who held him as if he might break.

Craig's nurse turned to her husband. "His eyes are clear."

"Get some blood."

"Okay?" asked Sam, having mastered the sounds in that word.

"Yes, Sam," Craig answered. "He has no outward sign of infection. I need a little of his blood to see if those strange cells are present. I'm done with Mary now. Give the baby to Casey for just a minute. What's his name?"

Sam gave his son back to Nurse Casey so she could draw a bit of blood. "Pen?" he asked.

"In the drawer." Craig pointed before he lifted Mary, and Caitlin's twin sister, Morgan, who also helped him, changed the linens for Mary to have a clean bed.

Sam found an old quill and ink writing combination. He grunted but figured out how to use it. On a piece of paper, he wrote: *Aidan Bartholomew Mercier.*

Craig read the name aloud once he'd placed Mary in a clean gown and bed. Casey handed the new mother her son. Mary caressed his head and smiled before she drifted to sleep.

Tongue-tied, Craig mumbled, "Are you a descendent of Bart and Keturah?"

"Yes," Sam answered and lay beside his wife. Within minutes, he, too, slept.

Renée O'Rourke stuck her head into the room. "All good?"

"More than good," Craig responded. "News on Sam's blood?"

"Yes. There are a few unusual cells, but nowhere nearly as many as the first batch of subjects."

Casey handed Renee another tube of blood. "Test this."

"Whose is it?"

Craig pointed at the baby. "Aidan Bartholomew Mercier's."

"Mercier?" asked Renée.

Craig nodded.

There were no odd-shaped cells in the baby's blood. Craig stared at a locked box in his office. *Is it possible?*

He stepped outside. "Brindle! I have a message for you to communicate to your granddaughter."

"I smell you!" Moonbeam groused as she flew low over Puma Pass. "But I can't feel you. What's hindering our bond, Aidan? Where are you?"

With a sharp pain, the dragon's thoughts mingled with another mind. "Grandpa! What's wrong?" Moonbeam shook her head. "Craig wants what?"

Brindle's voice sounded in the young dragon's head. "Political prisoners."

"I'll let Father know. And you want the two you mentioned in particular?"

"Yes."

"I understand." She laughed. "I know how much you hate linking over long distances. I love you too."

Submerged in the Potomac River, Smoke's eyes popped open just above the surface. "Craig wants who?" he asked Moonbeam.

She repeated what she had said.

"Shit, shit, shit!"

"Father!"

"At this very moment, Rennin is beating the shit out of him, but I'll invade his thoughts."

Six men held Rennin O'Rourke off Vice President Geoghegan. "Do what?" Rennin shouted. He turned around in a circle, shaking off his restraints and placing his hand to his temple. "Craig wants whoever is running the United States? He's got it."

Half-way around the world, Scarlet jerked awake. "Moonbeam, is everything all right?"

"Yes, Grandmother. Grandpa sent a message from Draconis. Craig wants a political prisoner—somebody named Kim Joowon."

"The Korean leader?"

"Yes."

"Why?"

"He wants to test his blood."

"But he's not even infected. He started bio-chem war."

"Maybe that's why Craig wants him."

"I'll let Ming know."

"Be careful, Grandmother. I have a bad feeling about that man."

Both beasts were quiet as emotional hugs coursed between them. Finally, Scarlet broke the silence. "Tell me what else is wrong."

"I can't feel Aidan, Grandmother. I'm frightened."

"Then it is time to listen with your ears."

"I will."

They broke the link. There was work to do.

"Aidan O'Rourke, right?" Nidia's voice boomed into the pit.

"Yes," Aidan affirmed.

"My father died when James Wilburn tried to kill yours. Our fathers were supposedly best friends."

"My dad told me about Jake Muñoz. You should know my dad killed James Wilburn."

"No great loss to mankind. But I have news for you. Apparently, your daddy is causing some kind of stir at the Pentagon. It seems you were right about the government. It also appears your little lady's grandpa is in the middle of the ballyhoo." She laughed.

"I told you that you would be my bargaining chips if I had to have some." She hoisted a ten-gallon bucket. "I wonder how much you're worth. Will they burn us up if some big shots' kids are part of us? I have a little surprise for you, Captain Moss. Let's see if the god-like creature you're with can save you."

Nidia popped the lid of the bucket and turned it upside down, giving it a hard slap to the sides. A rushing, roaring wave of brownish, reddish, blackish insects rained down upon the couple. Some flew. Others fell, landing on Aidan and Laurel, crawling over them, burrowing into their hair.

Laurel's screams reverberated, echoing throughout Puma Pass.

A cockroach raced across her mouth. "Oh, God! They were bitten by cockroaches? That can't be the source of contamination!"

Frenzied, Laurel ran around the deep cave, swatting her bound hands at flying bugs.

Aidan cleared a small cleft of any insects. "Come here!" he yelled. He slapped bugs off her and pushed her into the recess, covering her with his body. He felt the vermin run across his feet and up his legs. He tried stomping to keep them away and perhaps kill some.

A man's voice bellowed above, "What the hell did you do, Nidia?"

Nidia laughed maniacally. "I dumped roaches in there, Sergio. The brave little Navy flier is terrified."

"That is just evil!" Sergio leaned over the ledge. "I'm sorry. I'll get you out in a few minutes. The roaches are just roaches. They aren't poisonous."

Sergio stormed out of the cave to look for rope and harness. Nidia ran after her brother. He pointed angrily at her. "How could you?"

"I only wanted them to squirm. How was I to know she would freak out?"

"Aidan *O'Rourke*! He could be our salvation."

Large golden orbs surveyed the situation. Moonbeam had heard Laurel's shrieks of terror and Aidan's voice. She listened intently to the conversation between Sergio and Nidia.

A growl rumbled in her throat and a stream of smoke wafted upward from her nostrils.

All thought of concealment left Moonbeam's mind. She soared over the mutants who gathered to witness the sibling argument, casting a cooling shadow on an already overcast day. She swooped down and snatched Sergio into a massive talon.

Clutching him to her, she circled like a vulture. Her voice resounded. "Nidia! You have someone special to me. I have your brother. I propose a trade. *Or,* I'm *very* hungry. You caused me to miss meals looking for Aidan. Sergio would make a good snack."

20
Epiphany

Moonbeam landed with a thud on a rise above Puma Pass. She lowered Sergio to the ground.

First, he patted her leg. Then he began to dance around.

"You're real!" he exclaimed. He jumped up and down and hugged the dragon's leg. "You are real. I'm not crazy."

He stepped back. "You aren't really going to eat me, are you?"

"Of course not!" A spark shot from Moonbeam's mouth. "I only eat bad people. Maybe I should eat your sister."

"She's not bad. A little misguided, but not bad. By the way, how many people have you eaten?"

"None."

"So, you're bluffing!"

"I can always make Nidia my first."

Sergio pushed against the air with open palms. "Please don't. Listen, I read that old book, *Memoirs of Magic*. I believed every word. Quazel was evil incarnate. I think I've found a link between bio-chem and Quazel."

"Not possible. How? What?"

"Take me back down there." He pointed. "I'll get Aidan and Laurel out. I need to talk to this Craig."

"Humph!" Moonbeam looked over her shoulder at the town. "Laurel is terrified of those things called cockroaches. She might be scarred for life. Nidia needs a little scare, but"—She sighed—"I'm here to help. Did she tell you some bigwigs plan to burn you up?"

"Yeah. I have thoughts on that too. Aidan and you can really help."

"Fine. Would you prefer to ride on my back to return?"

"I would *love* that."

As people in Washington D.C. got their first look at a dragon when the Vice President was thrust into Smoke's talons, Cliff Spell grabbed his head. "Oh, my God!" he yelped.

Char sent him all the images Moonbeam had given him, and they instantly transferred to both Smoke and then Rennin.

Rennin and Cliff gawked at each other. Taking a deep breath, Rennin said, "Well, that explains a lot."

Cliff nodded. "And makes this mission even more important, nephew."

The two men embraced as Smoke lifted off.

Dr. Craig Jamison walked into his lab with the lockbox under his arm.

"What's that, Craig?" Renée asked.

D'Aubigné looked up from Petri dishes where she tried various potions on blood samples to test effects. "Why do you have that?"

"What *is* it?" Renée demanded again, more urgently.

Both women felt great agitation in their spirits.

"Relax," said Craig. "I have to test something. In here is the dirt from the floor of the cave where a couple drops of Victoria Reinhardt's blood dripped when Rennin ripped her heart out. When d'Aubigné incinerated her, three drops of blood remained on the floor. I remembered Victoria had used the few remains of Quazel to create the potion that brought her back within herself. I couldn't take a chance it could ever happen again. I scooped the drops along with the dirt from around them into a vial and sealed it. Then, I locked the vial in here. I told no one, not even Casey."

He set the box beside his stepdaughter. "D'Aubigné, when I open this, be prepared. I have a theory. On one hand, I hope I'm wrong. On the other, we can combat this if I'm right."

He took a small key from a pocket. "Are we ready, ladies?"

Moonbeam glided to a stop in front of Nidia who had not moved an inch. Other residents screamed and scurried to hide.

Scarcely above a whisper, Nidia said, "Oh, my God! You're real."

Moonbeam placed Sergio beside his sister. "Yes," he said. "You used to believe."

"I thought they'd come to save us." The words came out strangled by tears.

Setting her teeth in her dragon smile, Moonbeam said, "We have."

Laurel's muffled screams of, "Get them off me," still sounded from the pit.

"I'm trying," Aidan responded, frustration evident in his voice. "There are too many."

"Do you mind?" Moonbeam jutted her snout toward where Laurel and Aidan were captive.

Nidia shook her head.

Moonbeam barely fit through the entrance. "I'm here," she announced and stretched a talon into the hole.

Aidan thrust Laurel into Moonbeam's talon and jumped up beside her. The dragon put the humans out the entrance where both Sergio and Nidia cleared any cockroaches off them and cut the bindings on their wrists.

"Stand back," Moonbeam commanded.

From the opening to the cave, she let loose a steady stream of fire. Popping, sizzling, and squealing sounds flowed from the cave.

Moonbeam turned to face the humans. "Laurel, they might have survived radiation fallout, but not dragon fire." Then, she engulfed Aidan with her wings. "Don't you ever go off without me again! I couldn't sense you. I felt lost."

Aidan hugged her back. "Me too. It must be the radiation hampering our link *and* my gift. Sorry, but I knew you'd find us."

He looked toward Laurel where she leaned against a section of fence, gulping air and still shivering. "I'll be right back."

Aidan walked behind Laurel and placed a hand on her shoulder. Before he could speak, she turned and wrapped her arms around his waist. Sobbing, she laid her face against his muscled chest.

He held her close. "Sh. It's over. Laurel, I love you. I'm sorry I didn't protect you better."

She sniffled. "Shut up, Island Boy. I'll be your Sunrise every day for the rest of my life; just don't ever let me see another cockroach."

"I don't think I ever want to see another one either."

She took a deep breath and relaxed into Aidan's arms. "I love you, Aidan. I won't pretend otherwise."

After a short time, Sergio interrupted the lovers' epiphany. He introduced himself. Then, he said, "I need both—I mean all three—of you to come to my research facility."

"Mercier Memorial Hospital?" asked Laurel, recovered from her emotional outburst, but still having spasmodic shivers.

"No. I'm set up on Alcatraz. I figured the hospital might be a target after my experiments were sabotaged."

He turned to Moonbeam. "Would you mind taking us?"

"No."

A child's voice called, "Mom!"

Laurel said, "Take Hope too. If they strike, they think Alcatraz is deserted."

Nidia nodded. "Moonbeam, can you carry all of us?"

"No problem, but you can't go until you apologize."

"I'm sorry. Really. I thought you were here to do something bad, set Sergio back." She glanced toward Laurel. "I'm really sorry about the roaches. I didn't know you were so scared of them."

Laurel shuddered again. Aidan put his arms around her.

"We're good to go then," Moonbeam said. She held out talons and transported five passengers.

Once inside the old prison, Sergio said, "I want to show you something. Then, I need to meet your Craig."

He escorted them directly to his lab. "Look at these slides." Pushing some computer keys produced a series of slides side-by-side on the wall.

"The first five are from different infected people. See the weird cells?" He pointed. "Notice that some have more than others. The few I gave certain serums do have fewer abnormal cells, but nothing has

145

completely eradicated them. Those serums were the items destroyed when some quack doctor came in to help. That's what made Nidia so distrusting." He patted his sister's arm. "Now, look at the last two. The next to last shows cells taken from the remains of James Wilburn. His body was sent back here for burial. I exhumed him when my theory took shape. Can you tell the cells with the almost triangular shape and little points near the top are still moving although he's been dead for several years?" He walked to the wall and placed his hand on the last projection. "This last one, I took from the bones of one Ichabod, Ike, Banks, the man who forced your ancestor, Aidan, to mine gold at gunpoint."

"What?" Aidan asked, shocked. "They had the same gene or virus or *something*? And it's not dead even though the people are?"

"Yep," said Sergio.

"How can this be?" d'Aubigné asked. "The same strange cells are present in Victoria's blood as in all these infected people. The more severe the infection, the more cells. Scarier is that Victoria is dead, but those cells are moving."

She gawked at the slide again. "I swear that those things resemble a

baphomet  ." She paced. "I've tried dozens of potions. Nothing kills it."

"But this Sergio that Sam mentioned must have found something that helps," said Craig.

"Did he?" Renée asked. "Sam is a real sweetie. Could the purity of the spirit be the antidote?"

"Aunt Renée!" D'Aubigné hugged her aunt and stepmother. "I think you've got something there!"

As they talked, Smoke landed outside and called, "Craig, special delivery."

Craig raced outside. "Who is that?"

"Vice President Carson Geoghegan of the United States. He's running the country—You said you wanted the person running the country. The President is infected, and he's been keeping it quiet until he got a stronghold. He's had the President shipped off to Puma Pass, of all places. But he was trying to get world governments to annihilate all the places they call cities of refuge. He wants to kill all the poor people this stupid war has infected."

"No, I don't!" yelled the Vice President. "Only the ones that seem beyond help. That's why I sent Barbour to Sergio."

"Get me some blood now!" Craig ordered. "Then lock him in with the worst lot." He gave Geoghegan a look of utter contempt. "Maybe they'll eat him."

Half an hour later, Craig, Renée, and d'Aubigné took turns viewing a slide under an old microscope.

"I'll be damned!" Craig exclaimed. "I can't explain it, but if my next subject has these cells, I'm calling it *The Evil Gene*."

21

✐nsurgence

Spotlights, heavily armed guards in exorbitant numbers, electrified fencing less than a foot behind razor-wire, and Pitbulls as guard dogs gave Ming Spell Picard and Harvey Zane pause outside the fortress where Kim Joowon resided.

"Do you think he's a little paranoid?" asked Zane.

"No. A lot. And Craig is insane. First, samples of the compound used in the bio-chem weapons, which can only be found here, and now Kim himself for blood."

"Well, at least we can get both jobs done with one raid." Zane lowered binoculars. "Did he stipulate breathing?"

"No, but I think he wants him alive."

"So, what's the plan, oh, Stealth Queen? Scarlet is not so easily hidden as Char."

"That could be good. Broad daylight affront with a red dragon might scare the shit out of the guards. And she can eat the damned dogs."

"The dogs are innocent and not normal food."

She held up a finger. "I stand corrected. Okay. No harm to dogs." She pointed. "She can drop us on the roof, circle a few times, and scatter the guards. We can grab Kim, force some bio-chem from him, and drag his worthless ass back to the roof. Scarlet can pick us up, drop us with Esmeralda and Filigree, and shuttle the compound and the nutcase megalomaniac to Craig."

Zane stared at the petite Asian, who in her forties still looked twenty. "You know, at times you sound as cold as them, Ming."

"You know better."

"Yeah, I do. And I like your plan. Shall we shoot for mid-morning?"

"Yep." She grinned. "I have it on good authority that some folks have already seen Smoke and Moonbeam, and not necessarily those we intended.

As they went back to firm up their plan, she told him what Scarlet had relayed to her mind.

Zane mumbled, "Seems like an insurgence has begun."

Ten A.M., a huge cardinal beast circled at first high, then lower and lower. Frantic voices and pointing gave way to mass chaos as soldiers dropped weapons and fled.

"Piece of cake," muttered Zane.

"We don't have our prize yet," Ming reminded.

Dropping from the dragon's back, who went back to her undulating spiral, Ming and Zane made their way to the inner sanctum.

Kim watched the frenzy from a window. At the sight of an enormous red dragon, he stepped back, his almond-shaped eyes becoming full-blown spheres. He turned to run and came face-to-face with two intruders who had taken advantage of the pandemonium.

The Korean leader screeched in his native tongue and tried to run past Ming and Zane. Ming struck with a palm-heel to Kim's chest. He fought back with agility against two assailants and managed to get out the door.

Ming and Zane pursued him. He rounded a corner and slipped through a door. Ming flew after the Korean leader and found herself flat on her back as Kim performed a clothesline move on her.

Following close on her heels, Zane came through the door just as Kim spun around with a syringe, jabbing the needle directly into Zane's heart. He crumpled, clutching his chest.

Kim pulled the hypodermic from Zane and turned on Ming as she recovered from her blow and attacked her. The needle raked across her forearm, but she landed a punch to the bridge of Kim's nose.

Blood gushing, he fled the room. Zane gasped for breath as Ming knelt by her friend. "Scarlet, get the son of a bitch!" she screamed.

As the Korean leader bolted for an armored limousine, Scarlet swept him into her left talon. "Ming, I have him," the dragon called in a booming voice.

"Come on, Zane, move," Ming coaxed.

"Can't breathe." Blood leaked from a pin-sized puncture. His eyes began to cloud. "Tell Nicole I love her."

"Oh, no you don't!" Ming exclaimed, looking at the scratch on her wrist.

She hooked Zane under his arms and dragged him toward the ground exit, stopping only long enough to snag another filled syringe from a rack near the door. In the courtyard, she called, "Scarlet, help!"

Scarlet scooped both humans from Draconis into her right talon.

"Home fast," Ming said. "Send messages ahead. Zane's dying. Hurry, Scarlet. Kim injected Zane and scratched me with bio-chem. I feel weird."

Char, Smoke, and Moonbeam all yelped as a pain shot through their heads simultaneously.

"Oh, shit!" bellowed Moonbeam.

As the only dragon outside Draconis who could continue the relay, Moonbeam probed Brindle.

"I'm on it, sweet girl," Brindle said to his granddaughter's mind and soared to Craig.

Aidan placed a hand on Moonbeam. "You're terrified. What's happened?"

"Ming and Zane got Kim, but at a price. Zane's…dead." Her breath came in gasps. Giant tears dripped to the floor, causing a slight sizzle. "Ming has been infected. Apparently, Kim stabbed Zane in the heart with bio-chem."

Sergio surveyed his new friends. "This makes me certain my next idea is a must."

"What do you have in mind?" Aidan asked.

"Insurgence. Between those of us who can function and a few scaly friends, we can take over crucial cities and force some sort of cooperation and change."

"I'm in," said Laurel.

"Me too." Moonbeam added.

Aidan nodded. "Contact Smoke and Char. Let them know. Char needs to get Randall and Marshall home. Zane is their father."

Scarlet flew, oblivious to anyone spotting her. A number of times humans screamed and ran to hide, but she never slowed for any government to get a tag on her.

News agencies rushed to report sightings. Scientists conjectured the soaring thing with wings had to be some new aircraft, but no country took credit for such a device.

Without stopping, Scarlet deposited all her human cargo at Craig's feet. She had to rest, or she would be useless in the coming fight. She swallowed three grazing sheep in mid-flight and crashed in her cave and slept as if dead for the next two days.

Showing no mercy, Craig drew Kim's blood and locked him in a solitary cell. Zane had no pulse. His wife, Nicole, could not be comforted.

Only hours after Scarlet, Char arrived with Zane's sons who found their mother a basket case and their sister armed and ready to fight.

Ming's eyes had a fine film over them by the time they reached Draconis, but she remained coherent. She confined herself to the hospital to await what might come.

Craig called d'Aubigné and Renée to him. "He has the cells in abundance—more than anyone we've tested except the residual blood of Victoria. Now, I have to analyze the compound which is more than his blood, and d'Aubigné, I need you to help me work on an antidote. I refuse to bury Zane until we find one on the chance there's a sliver of hope. I've had him moved to the mountains where he can be basically kept on ice."

Craig walked out of his facility to a crowd, both human and dragon. "I see by now many of you have been called to the outside. Go do what you must do. As soon as I have something to share, I will."

As he finished speaking, Smoke landed with one more bio-chem mutant. Sergio Muñoz dismounted and introduced himself to Craig. "I've come to work *with* you, not against you, and not *for* you."

Ming stepped forward. "Does either of you think I'll get worse?"

"No," Sergio replied.

Craig jutted his chin. "You're needed out there. Go kick some ass."

Draco flew over. D'Aubigné looked skyward. "No, wise one. I need you here. It's not yet your time to go."

Within a week's turnaround, Alcatraz Island was swarmed. Ten dragons surrounded it as a great number of Draconians joined the mutants and a large group of military personnel led by Lieutenant Arjun Ralston. Treason meant little to him when it came to following his conscience and protecting his family.

Nidia faced the task of telling her daughter she had lied, and Hope met her father. Man and child wept.

Military officers, both young and mature, poured over maps. Target cities chosen, insurgent teams formed. Each team was made up of a dragon, at least one Draconian and one mutant, and a dozen military personnel from various countries, most from the country or general area to be targeted. Logistically, each team needed a person who spoke the language of the region. Communication among groups was both electronic and telepathic through dragon links.

At midnight on the day the United States celebrated its independence, the teams dispersed. Clifton Spell and Sylvester Bolton with Char converged on Washington, D.C. They hid near the Potomac to await the command of simultaneous attack.

Rennin O'Rourke, Peter Pryor, and Smoke took their squad to Ottawa, Canada. Moonbeam ferried Aidan O'Rourke and Tyler Bishop, d'Aubigné's husband, with a larger number of bio-chem sufferers than the other groups had to Denver, Colorado.

Because she spoke fluent Chinese, Ming Spell Picard took Nidia Muñoz and Scarlet, who was bonded to Ming, along with a great many military trained fighters, to Beijing. With her Celtic ties, Renée chose Sam Mercier to accompany her and Draco's mate, florescent green Esmeralda, to lead the takeover of London.

All of Harvey Zane's children joined the fray, partly to avenge their father. Randall Zane and Jacques Picard took Brindle, who, having a quasi-bond with Zane, felt a deep anger and need to help, and equal numbers of mutants and soldiers to Moscow while Sandy, Brindle's mate and surprisingly bonded to Nicole Zane, went with Marshall and Michelle Zane and their team to Buenos Aries.

Dragons Periwinkle and Rose chose to leave their world to help Rennin's twins who were married to the Zane brothers. Caitlin and Periwinkle had bonded as had Rose and Morgan. Athens, Greece, became Caitlin's assignment with Periwinkle and Bobby Willis. Morgan chose Arjun Ralston to go with her and Rose to Johannesburg, South Africa.

Finally, Laurel got her desire when Filigree agreed to be her bonded dragon. Along with Lieutenant Dale Stevens, and a select few others, they stormed the holy city of Jerusalem, with the Israeli diplomat's assistance. Jerusalem was easy as the country's leadership came aboard voluntarily. It was the ideal location to cover the entire Middle East.

With a kiss to her forehead from Clifton Spell, since she had insisted on coming to Alcatraz from Miami, Margaret Sanders was left to hold the fort with Hope Muñoz-Ralston at her side.

At exactly high noon Eastern Daylight Time, each dragon began a Biblical assault and circled their targeted city once a day for six days and then seven times on the seventh day. The screams of terrified citizens rang out worldwide. Without a single weapon being fired, each team took command of their targets at one P.M. Eastern Daylight Time on the seventh day, and the human commanders called press conferences.

Televised around the globe, Rennin O'Rourke declared from the unlikely target city of Ottawa:

"Negotiations of peace have begun. No more secret meetings designed to annihilate a people will occur. If one person who has been afflicted with mutations due to bio-chem is harmed, there are ten beings of untold power positioned around the world to wreak havoc on all offenders. More can arrive with a moment's notice. These gentle, peace-loving dragons—and I do mean *dragons*—will put a stop to mass murder.

"At this very moment, Doctor Sergio Muñoz, who I discovered was actually awarded a Nobel Prize for his research for a cure for bio-chem but couldn't go to accept it since he himself is a sufferer, and Doctor Craig Jamison on an island that until recently was only accessible via magic, yes, magic, are working to formulate an antidote for this plague you unleashed on one another. As soon as a cure is found, global administration will begin. Then, all, and I stress *all*, facilities that create weapons of mass destruction and poisoning will be razed.

"The world is asking who we are. We are Draconians. For centuries we have been hidden. That time is no more. We are now one world. We will not stand by and watch that world destroyed.

"Now go about your lives. I am Rennin Duncan O'Rourke, Governor of Draconis. Some of you may have known me as Troy Tomerson, a former Oakland Raider. I will give updates as soon as I have them. We have no desire to harm anyone. We wish to make the world a place where love and tolerance abound. No more death. No more killing. Give us that chance. Unite as one."

Rennin stepped away from the media. Smoke asked, "Are you all right?"

"I don't want power. I want this over, and I want to go home. If the world leaders agree, we'll send representatives to a new United Nations. If our efforts prove futile, we'll go into permanent hiding. Draconis will be its own world. If years down the road, they turn on us, we will close our doors forever and let them kill one another."

Smoke nudged Rennin with his snout. They needed no words.

22

The Purest Spirit

"**The** Evil Gene. That's what I call it," Craig said to Sergio.

"So, you found the same cells in the blood from a woman who consumed a concoction she made from the remains of the witch Quazel, just like I found in the remains of wicked dead people?"

"Yes."

"And in the Vice President's blood?"

"Yes."

"But he hasn't been exposed to bio-chem."

"Neither has Kim."

Sergio looked out a window. "So, Dr. Jamison, this strange mutated cell is the catalyst that catapults the other components into thrusting the human body to regress?"

"It would seem so."

"Have you isolated the other components?"

"Some of them." Craig rubbed the back of his neck.

"Let's pool what we know," Sergio said.

"Absolutely, but let's wait for d'Aubigné to get here. Some of the herbs she isolated."

"Of course. The reason we men of science have had such a hard time is that we've overlooked the supernatural element."

Craig prepared strong, hot tea while they waited for the third party who might have missing information.

D'Aubigné arrived with a bottle of her father's homemade whiskey. "I thought we might need something stronger than tea."

Craig poured three glasses. "I always do, every time I review the symptoms and see some of the subjects we have here."

"What have you observed, Craig?" Sergio asked, taking a swig of whiskey.

"Definitely increased aggression and hypersexual stimulation. Very Neanderthal behavior there. Of course, the vulnerability to light, the visual sensitivity and rapid cataract growth."

Sergio interrupted, "I think the rapid cataract growth is a defense mechanism by the body to protect the eyes. Though I have the film, my vision is not impaired as cataracts do."

"You could be right. I've noticed the lack of visual impairment; actually, night vision seems enhanced."

D'Aubigné listened intently as the two doctors talked, waiting to add her own observations.

Craig went on, "The hypertension at a deadly level and insomnia frighten me."

"Yes," Sergio expounded, "most deaths after the initial impact have been from cerebral hemorrhage and stroke."

"They eat constantly, but never gain an ounce. And the preference for blood and raw meat!" Craig shivered. "However, I have *not* seen any cannibalism. And the subjects that came with Sam want their meat cooked."

"Yes, Sam tried some of the possible antidotes I developed." Sergio pushed the whiskey aside and opted for tea with sugar and milk. "Sam could have been as advanced as I am if he hadn't run from the so-called doctor. He overheard him planning to abort Mary's baby."

Craig cocked an eyebrow and looked at d'Aubigné.

Sergio seemed not to catch the exchange and went on. "I found serums that countered some of the effects, but nothing that eliminated all of them and positively nothing that gets rid of the evil gene."

Craig took a swig of whiskey. "Well, I guess it's not really a gene. Little Aidan…"

"Aidan?" Sergio asked.

"Mary had the baby," d'Aubigné explained.

"She's here and has the baby?" Sergio's excitement rose.

"Yes, why?"

"I want to see her."

"Because?" D'Aubigné sounded like a protective mother.

"Is she all right?" Sergio relaxed at d'Aubigné's tone. He sensed her protectiveness. "She's my baby sister from Mom's second marriage."

Craig said, "Mary has some distinctively Asian facial features."

"Yes," Sergio agreed. "My stepfather was Rennin Li."

"Rennin Li?" Craig shook his head as if to dislodge water in his ears. "Perchance related to Chen Li, the partner of Rennin O'Rourke of Puma Pass Mining?"

"Direct line. And so, we can stop hem-hawing, let me tell you of my lineage. I have old journals, and a serving wench in Barcelona records having relations with a pirate—Ricardo Mendez-Morales. He never knew he left a little gift behind, another daughter. I am a direct descendant of Ricardo. My father's friendship with Troy Tomerson was destiny. All of it played to bring us to this point in time, a time when we must join to save our world."

D'Aubigné tapped the glass against her teeth. "I'd react just like you if this was Aidan we were talking about. I'd probably be more defensive than you are. Mary's fine, and so is the baby. Visit with her at the hospital after we do our jobs."

Sergio nodded. "Continue."

"The baby is named Aidan because Sam believed our Aidan came to help," Craig explained. "Apparently, the infection can't cross the placental barrier. Little Aidan has no mutations."

"And," d'Aubigné put in, "we know people unaffected have the odd cells."

"Hm. So, we need to analyze what's in the compound. It would appear Kim and others added their own blood to catalyze the other components," Sergio assessed.

"Yes, it would. Doctors, you've yet to mention the mental and psychological effects, the protruding frontal lobe and increased brain function." The mage looked from one man to the other. "Sam is hypersensitive to feeling, like Aidan. But Aidan doesn't have a physical abnormality to go with his empathic abilities. Last, are the hallucinations. I'm almost certain of two things we'll find. I think we'll find the chemical compound for, is it called LSD, Craig?"

Craig nodded.

D'Aubigné went on after the confirmation. "Ergot can be very powerful. That alone would be a negligible effect, even desired by some. Quazel used ergot to drug Alexander, Duncan, and Aidan centuries ago. Victoria used it during her ritualistic sacrifices. Many fungi have hallucinogenic properties, and ancient cultures used them in religious practices. Another naturally occurring chemical in the human body and many plants used in ayahuasca brews is called DMT. Craig, you can say the long scientific name." She waved a hand.

"Dimethyltryptamine."

"Anyway, I'm sure there will be traces of it in the formula. It's thought to awaken spiritual awareness and has been used for ages. I know for a fact that both Daddy and Aidan have high levels naturally in their system. So did Sam. Daddy can wave a hand and control the actions of weak-minded people. Aidan is very in touch with the spiritual realm, probably because of his heightened sensitivity. The problem is the combination of drugs, chemicals, poisons, and, I'll say it outright, demon blood."

"Demon blood!" both men exclaimed.

"Yes. Aunt Renée mentioned purity of spirit being a main antibody. Sam is a sweet and gentle soul. I have an idea, but let's break down the bio-chem first. If my thoughts prove true, and we test my serum on unaffected folks, like Kim, they might die." She shrugged. "No great loss. Or they might be freed from a form of possession. We'll have to see."

D'Aubigné cracked her knuckles. "Sergio, you found ways to help. Did you bring any kind of documentation we can look at?"

"Of course." He reached into a small briefcase he had brought with him. He spread several charts and the three of them looked over the paperwork.

Craig tapped a number of formulas. "These are chemical compounds that helped?"

"Yes." Sergio nodded.

"They're the same formulas d'Aubigné mixed naturally."

Sergio looked at the young woman. "Then, let's use the natural-occurring ingredients, although, if you think about it, most medicines have origins in nature."

"That's true," Craig concurred.

D'Aubigné stood. "Time to work, guys." She sashayed out, the emerald silk robe she wore swishing.

"She can be abrupt." Sergio pointed. "She's a witch?"

"A mage. Very powerful. If we can isolate the items needed, she'll create an elixir that will kick bio-chem's ass."

"She's beautiful, but there's something a little different about her. The way she's built."

Craig knitted his brows. "All O'Rourke women seem to be tall and lithe. The men are tall and very buff."

"That's not it." Sergio screwed his face up in thought. "I know." He snapped his fingers. "It's the tiny point on her ears. Aidan has it too."

"Okay, I noticed that as a cosmetic surgeon. They are of true Irish descent. Is it possible there's a bit of Fey, maybe Elf, in them?"

"Elf?"

Craig hooted. "Is it any harder to believe in elves and fairies than dragons?"

"No. It explains a lot. Let's help the lady."

Around-the-clock work with single drops of bio-chem yielded excellent results. D'Aubigné sat back and chugged a double of her father's whiskey. "Damn Kim! Some of these components by themselves and in the right dosage are beneficial. Sassafras, for example, works well as an analgesic, but concentrated oil renders the subject impervious to pain—sort of like that stuff Craig called PCP. I think the jerk wanted to create a super-soldier, and he used this on his own people. Those were the most highly altered subjects. When he saw it didn't render what he wanted, he used it as a weapon against his enemies who in turn made their own and retaliated."

"I agree," Sergio said. "Like you said earlier, folks who want to trip on DMT, LSD, or mushrooms, their business; but not if it's forced on a person. And the presence of strychnine, radium, and cadmium—a flagrant attempt at poisoning."

D'Aubigné nodded. "Khat is also natural and used by many tribes in ritual religious practice."

"Yeah, but then throw in the shit they called bath salts"—Craig shook his head and rubbed his temples—Methylmethcathinone, Cathinone, Methylenedioxypyrovalerone, and Pyrovalerone."

"I can't even pronounce that stuff, Craig," d'Aubigné said.

"Finally," Sergio added, "damn parasite spores—shit that takes over ants and grows out of their heads—Ophiocordyceps, a hyperparasite—add your demon blood"—He slapped his hands together—"Monsters!"

"Gents, I'm surprised there were any mutants. I would put money on countless dead with failed experiments."

"So, Mage d'Aubigné, can you come up with an elixir?" Sergio grinned.

"I think so. I have a secret ingredient to obtain. Get me several Petri dishes ready. I want one for every mutant, you too, Sergio, and Kim and Geoghegan." She stood. "I'll be back."

Walking outside, d'Aubigné called, "Draco, I need you."

In Alexander's Cavern, d'Aubigné mixed multiple herbs and brought them to a boil. She let them steep to form a tea. She added various oils to the formula.

All the while, Draco watched her. She turned wide green eyes on her bonded dragon—the eldest of his kind—the firstborn of a salvaged race. "Wise one, I need to add one more component to create a serum."

"What do you need, my girl?"

"The purest spirit."

A long silence fell between them. "I need a little bit of your blood," she said so softly only a dragon could hear.

Draco hooded his eyes. "There are only two places where a human syringe can possibly pierce my hide. How much do you need?"

"To formulate the initial elixir, only a vial. If it works, maybe a bit more, but only a drop should be enough for three cc's. I'm thinking when your blood mixes with the components I have, the cells will multiply as needed."

Draco nodded. "Get what you need."

D'Aubigné retrieved a large syringe. Draco lifted her in his talon to hover in front of his chest. He put a keen claw to a scale over his heart.

"Will it hurt?" he asked.

"It might sting."

Draco lifted the scale over his heart. D'Aubigné touched the soft skin beneath it. Quickly and with precision, she inserted the needle and filled the syringe with thick, sparkling, gold fluid. She withdrew the needle and placed a kiss on the small puncture. "All done." She clutched her chest. Her breaths were sharp gasps.

"It didn't hurt at all."

"I'm glad," she whispered.

"What did you do?" Draco asked, feeling her distress. "You took the sting onto yourself. Why?" Tears brimmed his eyes.

"I would never hurt you. I'm all right now. Really. Set me down."

Draco put her on the floor. D'Aubigné walked back to the simmering cauldron. She passed her hand over Draco's blood and invoked an incantation:

> *Fórsaí Ifreann Chomhrac ar.*
> *Briseadh banna Satan.*
> *Purge nimhe.*
> *Athchóirigh spiorad neamhchiontach.*
> *Tús a chur le saol as an nua.*
> *Athair ar Neamh,*
> *Beannaigh seo a chruthú.*
> *Olc undo.*
> *Glóir mise.*

> Combat Hell's forces.
> Break Satan's bond.
> Poison purge.
> Restore innocent spirit.
> Begin life anew.
> Father in Heaven,
> Bless this creation.
> Evil undo.
> Glory be yours.

Taking a deep breath, d'Aubigné added blood from the purest spirit she knew to the brew she had begun. Spit and sizzle heralded the finished product with a final stir. The color of the potion took on an amber sheen with a sparkle as the light refracted at the correct angle.

D'Aubigné scooped a cupful and covered the rest. "Take me to Craig, please," she requested.

Inside the research lab, she held out her offering and prayed for a miracle. "One drop in each dish," she instructed.

Craig and Sergio took the cup and began a systematic dispensation into the Petri dishes.

Minutes seemed like hours. Hours passed slowly.

"Bingo!" Sergio hollered, viewing his own blood through a microscope.

Craig pointed at his slides. "Kim's dead, but not Geoghegan. What's your secret ingredient?"

With a Mona Lisa smile, d'Aubigné replied, "It's a secret."

23

Bread and Honey

"**How** do we administer it, and who goes first?" Craig asked, enthusiasm pouring from him.

Sergio volunteered. "I'll go first."

"No," d'Aubigné objected. "Just in case it doesn't work the same on humans, we need you to help us keep researching."

Sergio scowled. "It has to work."

"I think it will, but let's test a few others first."

"Such as?" Sergio raised his eyebrows.

D'Aubigné looked toward her stepfather. Craig nodded. "The Asians. They're the worst off." He looked at the remaining bit in the cup. "This is awfully thick to inject, and where?"

"I thought we could mix it with honey and spread it on bread for them to eat," d'Aubigné suggested. "Honey is a neutral substance. Let's see if ingesting it will work before we start injections."

"How much do you have?" Sergio asked.

"A cauldronful right now." She rubbed her hands down her face. "I'd like to place an inexhaustible spell on it. I really don't want to take anymore…"

Craig stared at her. "What did you do?"

She held her hands out as if pronouncing a benediction. "*Rúnda riamh nochtann.*" (Secret never reveal.)

Both Craig and Sergio suddenly developed a case of cottonmouth. "Did you just curse us?" asked Craig.

"Only if you divulge the secret ingredient."

"You didn't tell us what it was." Sergio gagged and guzzled water.

"If you repeat what I tell you, no amount of water will quench your thirst. You will dehydrate and die."

"Oh, God!" Craig exclaimed. "It's Draco's blood, isn't it? The purest spirit. And he gave it willingly."

"Yes."

"Cast your spell," Sergio said. "We will never speak of this."

As suddenly as the thirst came on, it dissipated.

D'Aubigné flew back to retrieve the cauldron. Draco whispered, "Don't harm others to protect me."

"No harm will come if they keep quiet."

"D'Aubigné, remove the spell, but don't tell them you did."

She waved a hand toward the research facility. "*Bain curse: Craig agus Sergio.*" (Remove curse: Craig and Sergio.)

"Thank you."

"You truly are the purest spirit."

They went together to the cauldron. D'Aubigné circled the pot thrice and spoke:

Infinitus saturavi.
One titeann thiocfaidh chun bheith dhá.
Dhá thiocfaidh ceithre.
Fanann Pot go hiomlán
Go dtí teastáil níos mó.

Infinite replenish.
One drop becomes two.
Two becomes four.
The pot stays full
Until needed no more.

She caressed Draco's leg. "That should do it." She covered the cauldron and got a large honeypot. Lifting both items, she said, "Let's do this."

Upon her return to the lab, d'Aubigné found Casey with platters of warm bread. Her mother beamed pride. "Craig says the three of you might have an antidote, and you needed bread to put it on so those poor souls can eat it."

If Craig didn't tell her, he won't tell anyone. Draco's safe.

D'Aubigné poured honey into a bowl and dipped a cup from the cauldron. Within seconds, the missing amount replenished. She added the potion to the honey, and Casey helped coat the bread.

Bread in baskets, d'Aubigné, Casey, Craig, and Sergio went to feed one group of mutants where Vice President Geoghegan cowered in a corner of the containment pen. The bio-chem mutants reached for the food. D'Aubigne spoke rhythmic, almost lullaby-like, chants as she gave the potion-coated bread out:

Nuair a íslíonn an Highland creagach
As Coill Sleuth sa loch
Tá luíonn oileán leafy
Nuair a dúisigh Herons flapping
An codlatach uisce-francaigh;
Tá againn hid ár dabhcha Sí,
Iomalán na caora
Agus de shilin reddest goidte
Tar a shiúl, O leanbh an duine!
Chun na huiscí agus an fiáin
Le Sí, lámh ar láimh,
Chun an domhain atá níos mó iomlán de gol ná mar
is féidir leat a thuiscint.

I gcás na tonnta na gluaiseanna moonlight
An gaineamh liath dim le solas,
Far amach ag Rosa faide
Chos againn go léir an oíche,
Fíodóireacht damhsaí olden,
Lámha mingling agus amharc mingling
Till Tá an ghealach a glacadh eitilte;
Agus a fro againn leap
Agus chase na boilgeoga frothy,
Cé go bhfuil an domhan iomlán de Trioblóidí
Agus is mian leis a chodladh.
Tar ar shiúl, O leanbh an duine!
Chun na huiscí agus an fiáin Le Sí,
lámh ar láimh, Chun an domhain atá níos mó iomlán de gol ná
mar
is féidir leat a thuiscint.

Nuair a gushes an t-uisce wandering
Ó na cnoic os cionn Ghleann-Car,

I measc na linnte luachair
D'fhéadfadh sin gann bathe le réalta,
Déanaimid iarracht chun slumbering breac
Agus cogar ina gcluasa
Tabhair dóibh aisling unquiet;
Ag claonadh go bog amach
Ó raithneach a titim a gcuid deora
Thar na sruthanna óg.
Tar ar shiúl, O leanbh an duine!
Chun na huiscí agus an fiáin
Le Sí, lámh ar láimh,
Chun an domhain atá níos mó iomlán de gol ná mar
is féidir leat a thuiscint.

Away le linn tá sé ag dul,
An sollúnta-eyed:
Beidh sé a chloisteáil níos mó mbuaile
As na laonna ar an gcnoc te
Nó an citeal ar an iarta
Can síochána isteach ina chíche,
Nó féach ar an lucha donn bob
Babhta agus thart ar an mhin choirce-cófra.
I gcás a thagann sé, an leanbh an duine,
Chun na huiscí agus an fiáin
Le Sí, lámh ar láimh,
Ó domhan iomlán de níos mó ná gol
féidir leat a thuiscint.

"Music soothes the savage beast," Sergio said.
"Yes, it *does* help," Craig confirmed.
"What is it? It's beautiful."
"William Butler Yeats's 'The Stolen Child' in the Irish."
Craig translated each line from the old language though his voice was nowhere as melodic.

> Where dips the rocky highland
> Of Sleuth Wood in the lake.

There lies a leafy island
Where flapping herons wake
The drowsy water-rats;
There we've hid our faery vats,
Full of berries
And of reddest stolen cherries.
Come away, O human child!
To the waters and the wild
With a faery, hand in hand,
For the world's more full of
Weeping than you can understand.

Where the wave of moonlight glosses
The dim grey sands with light,
Far off by furthest Rosses,
We foot it all the night,
Weaving olden dances,
Mingling hands and mingling glances
Till the moon has taken flight;
To and fro we leap
And chase the frothy bubbles,
While the world is full of troubles
And is anxious in its sleep.
Come away, O human child!
To the waters and the wild
With a faery, hand in hand,
For the world's more full of
Weeping than you can understand.

Where the wandering water gushes
From the hills above Glen-Car,
In pools among the rushes
That scarce could bathe a star,
We seek for slumbering trout
And whispering in their ears
Give them unquiet dreams;

Leaning softly out
From ferns that drop their tears.
Over the young streams.
Come away, O human child!
To the waters and the wild,
With a faery, hand in hand,
For the world's more full of
Weeping than you can understand.

Away with us he's going,
The solemn-eyed:
He'll hear no more the lowing
Of the calves on the warm hillside
Or the kettle on the hob
Sing peace into his breast,
Or see the brown mice bob
Round and round the oatmeal-chest.
For he comes, the human child,
To the waters and the wild
With a faery, hand in hand,
From a world more full of
Weeping than you can understand.

D'Aubigné neared the Vice President.

"What's that?" Geoghegan asked, body pressed against the bars.

D'Aubigné cocked her head. "Bread coated with a possible antidote."

The Vice President held out his hand. "Give me some."

"You're not a mutant," said Craig.

"I heard what you said. I have a weird cell. I swear I wasn't being underhanded about the President. I didn't have the confidence I could lead. He was bitten by a mutant when he went to see the extent of the problem. It would have caused more fear if Americans had known. It took weeks for the symptoms to show. Saliva must not be as potent. Please?" He held his hand out more insistently. "I want to get rid of the cell. I am *not* an evil man."

"There's the difference, Craig," d'Aubigné said. "That's why his regular cells didn't die. Kim, I think, knows what he is and likes it, much like Quazel, Ike Banks, Victoria Reinhardt, and James Wilburn. They accepted the power that evil can give. They didn't want to change. We know a bite can do this. Stephanie was bitten as they crossed a river to safety."

She handed a piece of bread to Geoghegan. "If you die, it was your choice."

He nodded and bit into the bread.

Half an hour later, every mutant slept, something they had done sporadically since arriving.

Geoghegan yawned. "I'm not dead. Is that a good sign?"

"I think so, Mister Vice President," Sergio said. "Go to sleep. Hopefully when you wake up, the cell will be gone."

The night dragged for three who had work hard to cure the afflicted. Waiting near the containment pens, their heads drooped in slumber, and they jerked awake more times than they counted.

Near morning, Vice President Geoghegan screamed in agony and twitched in seizure. Craig rushed to him. After several minutes, the Vice President opened his eyes. "Is it over?" he croaked as if one with laryngitis.

"I need some blood," Craig said.

Geoghegan nodded weakly. "Take it."

As Craig went to the research lab to view the new blood sample, Sergio and d'Aubigne had to deal with screaming and seizing victims as each awoke. Craig returned to see the entire group sitting and holding their heads.

"Well?" Sergio demanded.

"No sign of the cells."

"Thank you, Jesus!" Sergio danced a little jig. "Let's test the rest."

Blood samples proved clean. Within twenty-four hours, outward facial and bodily distortions disappeared. Eyes cleared.

D'Aubigné wept. Craig hugged her. "Why tears, darling?"

"I'm happy."

"We have reason to rejoice," Sergio said. "Can we get on with the rest of us?"

"Sure," d'Aubigne said. "I'd like you, Stephanie, and Mary to be at the hospital in case your seizures should be severe. We know what to expect."

"Mary," Sergio said with tenderness. "I haven't even seen her yet."

"Well, get over there," d'Aubigne said. "I'll get Stephanie. She's with Grandpa. He won't let her out of his sight."

"Gerald's in love." Craig grinned.

D'Aubigné agreed, "Yes, he is. It's nice to see his smile, but he's worried sick and feels guilty." She waved her hands in a shooing motion. "I'll meet you there."

D'Aubigné arrived at the hospital with her grandfather and Stephanie Pitts to find Sergio cuddling his nephew and comforting his sister.

Mary reached for her baby and kissed his head when Sergio placed him in her arms. She held baby Aidan out to d'Aubigné. "You care if."

With a deep sigh, d'Aubigne took the infant and cradled him close. "You'll be fine, Mary."

Before any other victims were treated, three special sufferers received the antidote. As with the first group, the three slept soundly after ingesting the honey-bread solution. Again, they awoke with pain and seizures, and within twenty-four hours were perfectly normal.

Sergio held his sister close and wept with her.

Gerald McClarty touched Stephanie's face and then pulled her into his arms. "I never thought I'd see those beautiful blue eyes again."

"Gerald, why didn't you tell me you loved me?"

"I thought I was too old for you."

"No way. You are like vintage wine."

"I love you, Stephanie. Will you stay here with me?"

"As your wife?"

"If that's what you want."

"Then, yes. I need to tell you, though, that I did marry after you disappeared. Married and divorced—twice. No one compared to you."

"I hate to interrupt these tender moments," d'Aubigné called, "but there are others to cure."

She hugged her grandfather and Stephanie. "You two keep visiting." Then she went to Sergio and Mary. "Mary, do you want to nurse Aidan?"

"It's not too late?"

"No," said Craig from the doorway. "I'll just need to give you a couple of shots."

"Yes!" Joy bubbled from the young mother. "When will you help Sam?"

"Very soon," Sergio said, kissing her forehead again. "Now let me help our new friends."

Draco sent the results to Esmeralda and Filigree, who relayed the good news to the other eight contingencies, Filigree testing his link to Moonbeam for the first time, with great success. D'Aubigné, Craig, and Sergio continued administering salvation to all those who had been brought to Draconis.

Finally, only Kim was left. D'Aubigne approached the man with Sergio and Craig. "How do we get him to understand what we say? None of us speak his language," she said. "And for some reason, I can't cast a translation spell on him."

A laugh the young mage had heard more than once escaped Kim's throat. In perfect English he said, "I'll always find some who will serve me, and eventually I will destroy your kind and your precious dragons. I thought fairies and elves ran away centuries ago. Yet, some remnant remains mixed with human blood. Oh, how I hate you and your kind. Human side, so pious, so sanctimonious. The Fey side so perfect, so beautiful. Even now I have one waiting to launch a new substance, one unaffected by dragon blood." The throaty laugh was sinister. "I already made sure there are no unicorns around—those flawless creatures whose blood is a cure all—well, almost."

Fighting fear and anger and dealing with the revelation that she was, indeed, Fey and there were others, d'Aubigne said, "Mr. Kim, if you can hear me, you have to fight this demon. Otherwise, you *will* die."

Kim reached his hand toward the bread d'Aubigné held. In broken English and his own voice, he said, "Give. Wet die. Son wead. Act fast before..." He fell to the ground.

The other voice screeched, "Fool!"

Kim pulled himself toward the bars and snatched the bread from d'Aubigné.

"Wait!" she yelled. "You'll die."

"Yes."

Kim swallowed the bread.

Part Four

Living Legend

24
A Thousand Fires

Rennin O'Rourke screamed into a cell phone. "Cliff, we have to act now! The last message about someone ready to launch a new kind of bio-chemical weapon is serious."

"I know. I have seven more dragons en route, along with a number of our people. Let's all meet on Alcatraz and launch simultaneous attacks from there."

"Who else is coming?" He paced to and fro. Smoke watched, his head whipping back and forth.

"My grandson, C.D., Sergio, d'Aubigne, Jennifer Willis, Colin Jamison, Gerry Willis, and Vice President Geoghegan. He's cured."

"Okay. Good. And the remainder of the dragons are forming a protective barrier around Draconis, right?"

"Of course. Draco's seeing to that."

"Then, I'll see you in a few hours. I'd wanted the strike to be after the antidote, but we can't wait." He disconnected with unnecessary force.

Sixteen hours later, Alcatraz Island was packed. More joint military units from around the globe joined the previous activists.

Vice President Geoghegan addressed the throng. "Arjun Ralston, where are you?"

Thinking he was about to be arrested for treason, Ralston squeezed Nidia's hand. "I love you," he said and stepped forward.

Geoghegan gave a nod. "As acting President, I am promoting you directly to general and giving you command of the combined forces, answering only to four others besides myself. You are to work directly with Admiral Sylvester Bolton, retired Lieutenant Colonel Clifton Spell, Ambassador Rennin O'Rourke, and Ambassador Char in the absence of Supreme Draconian Ambassador Draco. Do what must be done."

He stepped away and went to the group he had just announced to be in charge. "I have to get to the White House." He rubbed his chin. "Remind me never to anger you again, Mr. O'Rourke."

"Rennin."

Geoghegan nodded. "I would ask for the loan of a flier, but I've arranged a pick-up. Thank you. Restore President Barbour as soon as possible." He shook hands all around, including a touch to Char's talon.

Once a helicopter lifted the Vice President out, Rennin took over. "Okay. We know where all the bio-chem labs and nuclear installations are, unless we missed the 'new' one. D'Aubigné!"

"What, Daddy?" she asked pushing through the crowd.

"Did you bring all the crystal charms?"

"Of course."

"Good. Since Craig stayed to deal with recovering victims, who should receive his and who should wear Zane's?" His voice broke a moment at the feeling of loss of a friend.

"I think Sergio should use the ruby. He and Craig are much alike." She gave the ruby talisman to Sergio. "And give Michelle Zane her father's topaz."

"Neither of his sons?"

"No. Trust me. They're good men, or I would never have let my sisters marry them; but Michelle, maybe because she was born on Draconis, is the dynamo."

"Do you remember who gets the others?"

She touched her chest. "You talkin' to me?" She handed the emerald on a gold chain to her father. "Here's yours."

"Thanks, smarty pants. Pass out the others and then scry for any facility we missed."

"Right away." D'Aubigné turned to Cliff and handed him the onyx. She found Renée, Jacques, and Ming and bestowed the sapphire, diamond, and opal.

She sought out Michelle and gave her Zane's stone. The girl cried. Sergio Muñoz stared at the petite redhead as she slipped the talisman on. D'Aubigné returned to her father with his amulet in her hand. He pointed. "Give it to Aidan."

"Yes, sir."

D'Aubigné found her brother wrapped around Laurel. She held up a hand. "I won't ask."

The couple laughed. D'Aubigné handed the amulet to him. "Daddy said to give it to you."

"Already?"

"You need the discernment."

"Okay." Aidan took the medallion and slipped the chain over his head. He ran his finger along the writing. बिजली की आंख के घेरे में "The eye in the circle of power." The untold thoughts he had learned to tune out became crystal clear, and he was able to focus on only those he needed to hear. "Awesome."

His sister took his hand. "I need you to help me scry. I think once I get a vicinity, you'll be able to lock on." She stared at Laurel. "You too. The power of three."

D'Aubigne procured the same map her father and Cliff had looked at in Bolton's office. In the center, she placed a white candle and lit it. She arranged four stones in the four directions, north, south, east, and west: hematite for Earth, blue calcite for wind, sunstone for fire, and blue aventurine for water.

With a multi-faceted pietersite on a solid gold chain dangling from her middle finger, d'Aubigné held her hand over the flame. She nodded to Aidan. He placed his hand on top of hers. He in turn nodded to Laurel.

Laurel hesitated. "I don't know how to do any kind of magic."

"Sure, you do," d'Aubigné said. "You have O'Rourke blood and you're Fey."

"Fey?"

"Fairy. You're too short to be Elf. And there's no point of any kind on your ears."

Aidan touched his own small point.

D'Aubigne nodded. "That's right, little brother. We have Elven blood—well, we're Fey and our manifestation is Elven. Laurel is smallish, so I'm guessing Fairy."

"Like Tinkerbelle?" Laurel's voice was shrill.

"No. Fairies are not tiny creatures that flit around like butterflies. They can be formidable. Winged, yes, but not little sparkling things, and their wings can be retracted. It's recorded that Priscilla O'Rourke was called a sprite. I think she *was* a Sprite, or part Sprite at least. I found old writings from before Alexander's time, mostly written in Gaelic." She shook her head toward her brother.

"I have no clue how they ended up on Draconis, but one day I found them among all the other magical writings. I had never seen them before. It's recorded that Duncan discovered Priscilla asleep in a boat and that she related having come from the Shetland Islands, but she knew nothing about her parents. There was a notation of strange ridges between her shoulder blades and spine. I'm certain they were in place for wings that never developed. She was a water Sprite, perhaps born of a human female who never told her and placed her in a boat, hoping for someone to find her and save her."

Aidan's mouth fell open. "Stop catching flies," his sister said with a smirk before continuing her explanation. "Even older than that journal entry by Duncan, was the fact that Alexander's grandmother was considered a raving lunatic. When as a very young maiden she came up pregnant, she insisted that a tall, lean man with long black hair, green eyes, and points on his ears—much larger than our little protrusions—came through shimmering air and seduced her. He had to have been an Elf. Aunt Renée has often been compared to a pixie because she has pixie blood or gifts. She's neither tall nor short; nor does she have pointy ears, but she does know magic, especially herbs. And she has O'Rourke blood. It could be she's what would be considered a Halfling. I think soon we'll all know, but right now, I need your help. Just put your hand on Aidan's and concentrate on facilities that produce bio-chem. Hopefully, if the demon wasn't lying, something not already highlighted will show up on the map."

Laurel placed her hand on top of Aidan's. D'Aubigne began a chant: "Aimsigh. Nocht gcás ina dwells substaint olc." (Locate. Reveal where evil substance dwells.)

The crystal began a slow orbit around the flame. Before long, Laurel took up the chant with d'Aubigne. Then Aidan joined.

Simultaneously, two miniscule fires erupted on the map, one in the middle of the Pacific Ocean and one in the middle of the Atlantic Ocean.

"Admiral Bolton!" Laurel cried. "Come quick!"

The admiral rushed to the three scryers. "What?" he asked.

"Can we get a ship or sub here and here fast?"

"Shit!" Bolton made calls in rapid succession. He came back. "The Brits are sending a sub to the coordinates in the Atlantic, and we have one on the way too. Japan is meeting us in the Pacific. We'll need to coordinate our dragon strikes with the subs."

"Whose ships are these?" Laurel asked, indicating the non-consuming flames.

"As near as we can tell, they're unmanned drones."

"Will the presence of subs trigger them?" Aidan looked worried as he spoke.

"I don't know," Bolton answered.

"Shit! Moonbeam!" Aidan grabbed his sister's hand and pulled her. "You'll have to create a barrier."

They mounted Moonbeam and flew as fast as the dragon could go toward the position of the danger in the Pacific. "There!" Aidan pointed after several hours.

"I see it." D'Aubigne spoke a spell:

Sciath thuas.
Urlár thíos.
Babhta agus cruinn.
Áit le dul.

Shield above.
Floor below.
Round and round.
Nowhere to go.

A shimmer in the air was the only evidence anything had happened.

"That won't stop the submarines, right?" Aidan asked.

"No. Whatever firepower they have will go through. Now, for the other one."

Moonbeam turned with the agility of a hummingbird and zoomed to the other automated drone. Upon arrival many hours later, d'Aubigné placed another bubble of protection over it, and the three flew to Miami to rest.

"Aidan!" Moonbeam called outside Margaret's home.

Aidan and d'Aubigné emerged disheveled and groggy.

The dragon hovered above the house. "Grandfather says we can stay here. The strikes are planned for dawn tomorrow. Our target is in Cuba. That's not much more than two wing flaps away. I really need to eat now and then nap some more. You two do the same. I'll wake you when it's time."

"Good deal, Moonbeam." Aidan rubbed her snout affectionately when she bent her head down. He and his sister returned to sleep.

Moonbeam found several deer before she slept some more.

Before daylight, Aidan and d'Aubigne raided Margaret's cupboard and gorged themselves on canned vegetables, dry Cheerios, and various canned meats.

Moonbeam arrived just before dawn and called them out. Cuba lay only a quarter hour's flight for a dragon.

Around the world at seventeen locations, magnificent beasts in an array of colors circled targets, humans from Draconis and outside nations and bio-chem victims nestled securely on their backs. In Earth's two largest oceans, submarines converged on two launch drones with rockets pointing in four directions. At exactly 0:600 hours on the anniversary of the 9/11 attacks of 2001, which many believed to be the beginning of World War III, electronic and telepathic orders went out. "FIRE!"

All over the globe, news agencies reported:

"It appears a thousand fires erupted at the same moment. The power of dragon fire consumed every facility that produced either nuclear or bio-chemical weapons. These creatures were assisted by a united coalition of countries, and two launch drones preparing to fire a different kind of deadly virus were destroyed in both the Atlantic and Pacific by combined American, Japanese, and British subs. We have been told the fires will burn until every scrap of material is ash and will then go out on their own.

"Anyone listening can hear cheers worldwide. International leaders state, 'It's over. Now is the time to rebuild and come together as one world.'"

25
ꟷ̄ealing ꟷ̄agic

Avoiding collision with helicopters, both military and media, dragon after dragon returned to Alcatraz Island. Grins plastered their faces, as well as the faces of the humans who slid from their backs.

Among the commotion and celebration, Nidia, with Hope in tow and Arjun close on their heels, found d'Aubigné. "I'm ready," she said, grasping the mage's arm.

"Wait!" Arjun shouted, worry etching his tightly knit brow. "What if it doesn't work outside Draconis?"

"Why wouldn't it?" Nidia argued.

"It's magical healing," Arjun said. "I don't want to lose you and Hope."

"Maybe you just want us to stay this way so you can control us."

"Stop, Mom," Hope said, near tears.

"Yes, stop," d'Aubigné reiterated. "I see no reason the antidote should *not* work here, but General Ralston's concern is real, Nidia. He loves you and his child. He's simply worried."

She turned to Arjun Ralston. "Someone will have to be first. I'd like some of your blood to be sure there's nothing dormant there, like the Vice President."

"You think I might have the cell?" he asked, sudden fear written on his face. "Please take it all if you do. If I survive, so will my family."

D'Aubigné patted his arm. "All right." Then she called Sergio and explained the situation to him.

Sergio said, "You know where to find my lab, Arjun. I'll meet you there in a few minutes."

With a nod, Arjun walked away. Nidia and Hope followed him.

"You don't think he has the cell, do you?" Sergio whispered to d'Aubigné.

"No, but if he thinks he's cured…" She shrugged.

Sergio laughed. "Maybe we should test a few severe cases to be sure he's *not* right."

"Okay. Do you have any subjects here?"

"Of course. Did you bring the cauldron?"

A head shake and a smirk was followed by, "If I weren't married, Dr. Muñoz, you would be a temptation. You saw me put it in your lab."

"But you *are* married," said a voice behind her.

She turned around into a hug from her husband, Tyler Bishop. "That I am, to the most handsome and fantastic man alive."

Tyler's blue eyes twinkled as he dipped his head to kiss d'Aubigné. His long brown hair curtained them for a semi-private moment.

Sergio cleared his throat. "I sort of have my eye on that gorgeous Michelle Zane. Is she taken? I really like redheads."

Both d'Aubigné and Tyler laughed as they bumped foreheads. "No, she's not taken," said Tyler. "I would've thought you would've been the one attached." The two men shook hands, but a shadow crossed Sergio's face. "Michelle is only eighteen," Tyler finished.

"What's wrong?" d'Aubigné asked, noticing the slight frown.

Sergio explained, "I was married. My wife died, along with our unborn child."

"I'm sorry," Tyler said.

"Me too," Sergio said, "but life goes on, and thanks to your wife, we have a real future ahead."

"And I'll introduce you to Michelle," d'Aubigné said.

"No potions or spells. I'd like any attraction to be real."

"On my honor." She kissed Tyler again and hooked her arm around Sergio's. "Let's get Arjun's blood and make sure this antidote works outside Draconis."

D'Aubigne took a step back from the subjects Sergio prepared to serve bread coated with honey and elixir. "Dear God!" she exclaimed. "They're worse than the Asians we had."

"Yes. They survived a direct hit. Nothing I tried helped any of their symptoms. They really aren't quite human anymore."

Several of the victims growled at Sergio. He sighed. "They don't recognize me. D'Aubigne, will you sing?"

"Sure."

She began a Celtic lullaby. As on Draconis, music soothed the agitation. The subjects snatched bread and ripped into it. Several threw it down after a few bites.

Sergio looked at d'Aubigne. "They'd rather have raw meat."

"No." She shook her head hard. "I don't want any other blood to mix with Draco's."

"Do you think a couple of bites will be enough?"

"We'll have to see. We might have to sedate them and inject them."

Only three bio-chem sufferers fell asleep. Without further ado, Sergio retrieved a dart gun and fired ketamine into another half-dozen. Before d'Aubigné could object, he used a syringe large enough for a thick formula like penicillin and injected those six directly into their stomachs.

"Does the name Dr. Josef Mengele mean anything to you?" d'Aubigné asked.

"Yes. He would've created this shit." He grinned. "I'm trying to help. I think you could see reasoning was out of the question."

"Okay." She raised her hands in surrender. "Let's hope it works."

As the bio-chem victims slept, Sergio drew some of Arjun's blood. He and d'Aubigné did, indeed, view it under a microscope.

"Clear," she said.

"Yeah. He's a good guy." Sergio smirked. "He just needs to marry my sister."

"Stop whispering!" Arjun called. "I can handle whatever news it is."

"You need to make an honest woman of my sister." Sergio gave the other man a lopsided grin.

"I will as soon as I can. That is, if I live."

"You're fine," Sergio informed. "We're testing the antidote on the direct hits."

"So?" Arjun glared at d'Aubigné. "You lied to me?"

"No," she said. "I needed to be sure you were clear. What if there *had* been the demon blood cell? What if it *was* controlling you to try and keep Nidia and Hope prisoner?"

"Okay. I get your point. So? Now what?"

Sergio said, "We wait long enough to see if the worst victims heal."

"Twenty-four hours?"

"Maybe a little longer considering their severity."

"Be patient," d'Aubigné encouraged.

A day later, the three victims who had eaten the bread awoke with the same reaction as those treated on Draconis. Seizures came, and then gradual recession of physical manifestations gave way to normal human beings.

However, those who had been injected still slept.

Sergio began to pace, concern flowing from his person.

Feeling the serious distress, Aidan came to him and placed a hand on his shoulder. "Relax. We know the cure will work for most folks. Would it be better for these to live as they were or to pass to peace?"

"What are you suggesting?"

"Nothing. Just consider their suffering."

"There was so much pain," Sergio said thoughtfully. "For me, the headaches were the worst. Migraines on steroids." He rubbed his temples at the memory. "I stayed awake for days before I'd crash and sleep just a few hours. But I put my time to good use. I isolated compounds and found *some* relief."

"You were affected residually."

"Yes. My wife died in my arms. She was seven months pregnant. I tried to deliver the baby by Caesarean, but she was dead too. Some of their blood got on me since I had no gloves."

Aidan patted Sergio's shoulder. "Don't beat yourself up. You did a lot, all you could." He bit his lip. "You used a tranquilizer on these, right?"

"Yes."

"Maybe that's the reason for the slower progression."

"The ketamine?" Sergio nodded. "You could be right. Thanks for the pep talk."

A groan from one of the severely affected grabbed their attention. "Get help," Sergio instructed. "If their seizures are extreme, we can't handle it alone."

Within minutes, Aidan had summoned a team. Those awakening experienced worse seizures than any thus far. Soon, they quieted and relaxed. Line by line, scar by scar, disfigurations ebbed.

Not knowing who he hugged, Sergio grabbed the nearest person. A moment later, Michelle Zane pushed him gently away. She laughed. "D'Aubigné said you wanted to meet me. That's some first greeting."

"Sorry. I got overly excited."

"No problem." She stifled a sob. "Too bad it wasn't soon enough for my dad."

Sergio cocked a brow. "We'll see."

Her eyes grew big.

He shrugged. "I haven't heard a calorically challenged female sing yet. D'Aubigné's rather thin and shapely. "

Michelle laughed. "And she sings beautifully."

Nidia caught her brother's hand, interrupting the moment. "Please? Now it's our turn."

Sergio nodded. "Let's get folks to Mercier Memorial Hospital for massive treatments. You, Hope, Sam and President Barbour first." He glanced back at Michelle. She waved him on with a smile.

After bio-chem victims in Puma Pass and the nearby areas received antidote, teams dispersed to camps around the globe to administer magical healing. Within a week, President Barbour returned to office.

Months went by. Only stragglers in small numbers still carried the evil gene. When one wandered up, treatment was immediate. Search and rescue teams worldwide began to seek any victims left. When found, they were transported to Mercier Memorial Hospital where doctoring of contaminated people continued.

Aidan came to his sister's side. "Hey. I think medical personnel can do this now."

"I suppose. Why do I feel the need to do more?"

"It's the land that needs you now, not people.

She stared into his matching jade eyes. "God! I feel it."

"Yes. Nature is calling you."

"Yes, but more." She held up an index finger. "Much more."

"One step at a time, big sister."

D'Aubigné nodded. "I need to go to that mountain where you camped."

"Moonbeam's waiting. Laurel and I are coming too. Just in case you need the power of three."

She stopped in her tracks. "I need the power of seven."

"What?"

"The charm holders have to go with me."

"I'll round everyone up."

She caught his hand as he started away. "I still need you and Laurel. And Tyler for moral support."

"You got it. I'll get Filigree too."

She smiled. "Close enough to Draco."

As the group started to leave, Hope Muñoz-Ralston and Sam Mercier joined them and asked to go. Without understanding why, d'Aubigné permitted them to go along.

A couple of hours later, Moonbeam and Filigree delivered Aidan, Rennin, and Renée O'Rourke; d'Aubigne and Tyler Bishop; Jacques and Ming Picard; Michelle Zane; Sergio Muñoz; Clifton Spell; Laurel Moss; Hope Muñoz-Ralston; and Sam Mercier to Pikes Peak.

Restored to look like an Egyptian princess, Hope tugged d'Aubigné's hand.

"What is it, sweetheart?" d'Aubigné asked.

"You need four more dragons."

Mage and child locked eyes. "You have the gift," d'Aubigné observed. "You're right. I see the configuration I need now."

"I heard," said Moonbeam. "I'm calling Father, Grandfather, Grandmother, and Grandpa right now."

Two more hours passed. The sky began to lighten in the east before Smoke, Char, Scarlet, and Brindle arrived.

D'Aubigne took stock. "Good. Everyone's finally here. For a spell this big, I must have every mind focused on healing Earth. I'll need a

huge variation of the Star of Magen 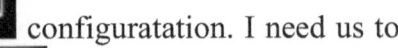 configuratation. I need us to

create a Sun-Moon Merkaba Mandala within a circle of healing herbs. I require the seven charms strategically placed in the circle. Work with me to get this done by dawn."

She took a bowl from a pack on her back. Then she retrieved thirteen leather pouches of healing herbs. In the bowl, she mixed tumeric, cinamon, garlic, rosemary, oregano, dill, cayenne, cilantro, mint, curry, rosemary, basil, and ginger. Into each hand she scooped the mixture, and turning three times, she pronounced an incatation:

Tá ciorcal foirfe timpeall orainn anois.
Le draíocht leighis, endow dom.

A perfect circle surround us now.
With healing magic, me endow.

A perfect circle etched in the ground all around the beings on Pikes Peak. D'Aubigne blew into her palms and the herbs floated on the air to fill the one-inch deep circle.

She clapped her hands, and seven points of light sprang from the circle at exact intervals.

"Quickly," she said, "place the enchanted gems at the lights."

Each person with talismans found a light and laid their charm at that point.

D'Aubigne nodded. She clapped her hands again. Six points of light appeared. "My dragon friends, please take a point. Face outward with your noses pointed skyward."

Each dragon stood on a bed of light. Rather than disappearing, the light bathed the ancient beings in a warm golden glow. Small curls of smoke rose from the dragons' nostrils, particles of moisture sparkling in the light. Gleaming lines formed a six-point star connecting the beasts. Then an oval of pure white outlined the creatures and joined at the center to make the flower of life with an ever-fluctuating iris in all the colors of a prism about two-feet in diameter.

Another hand clap produced twelve points of light. "Pick a point," d'Aubigne instructed the humans with her. Once each person had stepped onto a pinpoint, a tangerine arc formed over each, intersecting all others in a ripple effect until a circle of arches was made.

At the next clap, the twelve signs of the zodiac emerged one at a time alternating with the twelve animals of the Chinese zodiac on twenty-four prickles of light: Aries, rat, Taurus, ox, Gemini, tiger, Cancer, rabbit, Leo, dragon, Virgo, snake, Libra, horse, Scorpio, goat, Sagittarius, monkey, Capricorn, rooster, Aquarius, dog, Pisces, pig. They all alternately shimmered in either blue or red radiance.

Then she placed the four elemental crystals at the points of the compass and stood on the fluctuating dead-center of the Merkaba.

In position, d'Aubigné raised her hands skyward and in of voice of prayerful supplication spoke:

Cara nó namhaid, ní ábhair sé
Beir chun cuimhne cad a bhí dearmadta agat.
Flóra ag dearadh soilse
Fána teacht amach agus shine.

Friend or foe, it matters not
Bring to mind what was forgot.
Flora by majesty design
Fauna come forth and shine.

The sun topped the mountains with rays as spotlights. Thunder rumbled. The ground shook. A scent as fresh-mown grass wafted on the air.

Total silence, complete still engulfed the mountain. A flash so bright it blinded and then nothing out of the ordinary caused each being to look at the others.

There were no vibrant auras, no sparkling entities, only thirteen humans and six dragons. The small cell phone Clifton Spell carried blared. He answered.

Margaret Sanders's voice squealed, "Cliff, the brown grass is green!"

D'Aubigne sank to the ground. Renée pulled her up. "No time to rest. We must repeat this on Salisbury Plain, but you'll need to stand smack dab in the middle of Stonehenge, day after tomorrow at the Summer Solstice Sunrise."

26

One More Chance

The entire group arrived at Stonehenge two nights before the summer solstice. It appeared the press had caught wind of the magical healing achieved in the Western Hemisphere and were on hand to capture the proceedings for the other half of the world.

In a voice amplified by enchantments, d'Aubigné announced, "If you stay, you must remain far away. You cannot be inside the circle that will form."

In a softer voice she said, "I am so tired. We *all* must rest and eat to have energy for another Merkaba."

A commotion nearby drew attention. Townsfolk from surrounding areas appeared with platters of food, a truckload of live farm animals, and blankets and pillows.

"I don't believe it," Aidan said.

A young woman being pushed toward the group dipped her head in a bow of subservience.

Aidan said, "Don't do that."

Barely above a whisper, the girl said, "Sorry, sir. I felt your needs." She made eye contact with Aidan. "For many years I've been called crazy." She looked back at the crowd. "Now, they know I'm gifted. We've brought food for all and a semblance of comfort for sleep."

"Were you the only one brave enough to speak to us?"

"They"—She pointed—"Felt since I'm like you, I would be the best candidate."

"Thank you. We greatly appreciate the nourishment." He walked with the girl to a self-imposed perimeter. Hope caught up and took Aidan's hand.

"Good thinking," he mumbled. "You're not scary at all."

The little girl giggled.

The three of them brought food back to the humans. Aidan turned to the bearer of the offerings. "What's your name?"

"Sabrina Danaher."

"There's no way you can be related to Diggory."

"Perhaps distantly."

He cocked an eyebrow. "You know who I mean?"

"Aye."

"Good then. Take the animals to that secluded area." He inclined his head. "Let the dragons eat in private."

"It is done."

Sabrina returned to give instruction, and Aidan told the dragons where to go. Half an hour later, all stomachs were filled.

Celtic guardians formed a circle snout to tail and the humans bedded down in safety.

Before daylight, electricity in the air crackled.

D'Aubigné bolted to her feet. "It's time." She waved her hand, and bedding sailed hundreds of yards away.

Feeling, more than seeing, the press of the media, d'Aubigne held her arms out from her sides, forming a cross. In a tight, dizzying twist, she set up a whirlwind. It spread out and out, pushing all but those needed for the healing spell out of the way. Once the proper distance was set, the cyclone spun, keeping all back. They could see through the winds but could not cross the barrier.

Once again, the young powerful mage performed incantations beginning with the circle of healing herbs. When all was in place, she took her position on the flower of life that had formed dead-center of Stonehenge.

When d'Aubigné finished the final chant, the flower of life continued to swirl. She stood her ground as the onlookers saw her engulfed in a constant flame burning blue-white, but not a hair on her singed. The ground around those in the flower of life trembled. D'Aubigné herself began an uncontrollable eddy, her hands held up as if in supplication. Words in a language she never spoke, not Irish or Gaelic or Latin, poured from her lips:

Adlam yr awyr.
Ail-lunio'r dwfn.
Revive y tir.

Adnewyddu'r ysbryd.
Iawn am y plentyn.
Adfer yr enaid.
Aileni y dyn.

Rebound the sky.
Reshape the deep.
Revive the land.

Renew the spirit.
Redeem the child.
Restore the soul.
Rebirth the man.

Beyond the last circle, another appeared as if in a synchronized wave. The Celtic zodiac—stag, cat, adder, fox, bull, seahorse, wren, horse, salmon, swan, butterfly, wolf, hawk—thirteen elements rose from the pulsating earth. Fire and spinning ceasing, d'Aubigné leapt away from the iris as a fluctuating portal ascended. A defined doorway appeared and then melted away. The air over the flower of life shimmered in waves as heat off hot pavement. The center shrank bit by bit until only a pinpoint of prismatic light was left.

The charge in the circle prickled the skin of man and beast. All stepped back a few feet.

A slurping sound yielded three tall, slender people, a man with two women flanking him. The women held longbows with arrows nocked. All three wore leather tunics over leather pants and boots. Their hair hung to the smalls of their backs; green eyes sparkled. Very pointed ears protruded through raven black with silver streaked hair on the man and blonde hair on the women.

The male made eye contact with Rennin, Aidan, and d'Aubigné.

"Ah, wyrion." ("Ah, grandchildren.") He bowed low and then tapped the hands of the women who lowered their weapons. "Yr wyf Arawn." ("I am Arawn.")

Rennin touched his daughter's shoulder. "What did he say? It's not Irish. It sounds like what you just spoke in that last incantation."

Arching an eyebrow, she asked, "I spoke a different language?"

Her father nodded.

"No, it's not a language I know." She spat into her hand, made a fist, and as if rolling dice, cast outward. "Teanga anaithnide; teanga a thaispeáint." ("Tongue unknown; language be shown.")

"Da iawn," said Arawn. ("Well done.")

"It's Welsh," d'Aubigne said.

The translation spell worked for all understood Arawn.

"*What* are you?" Rennin asked, a lump in his throat.

Arawn laughed, the sound melodic. "I am Fey—Elven King to be exact. Are my kind now welcome in this world? Behind me is another realm—Faerie Keep. Many magical beings reside there: Fairy, Elf, Sprite, Halfling, Dwarf; and animal kind—Unicorn, Merfolk. I see the Ancient Ones are with you." He frowned. "But these are not ancient."

Char bowed his head to the Elf King. "I am Char, the second eldest of a salvaged race. There is much to tell."

Hand held out, Arawn said, "May I?"

Char lowered is head and Arawn touched the soft spot behind the dragon's eyes. The shared and inherited memories poured forth. After a time, the Elf King stepped back. "Yes. It is time for our return. We will give this world one more chance." He pointed at the thirteen people. "I wish you to come with me." He smiled toward d'Aubigne when she scowled. "Your barrier will remain in place until we return, and this gateway will stay open. We will once again walk among you." He furrowed his brow and pointed at Filigree and Moonbeam. "You two come also."

Arawn turned to his guards. "These are Ynyra and Cerys, my daughters." To them he instructed, "Stay here in case something should occur."

He stepped aside and indicated with his hand. "Come."

The two youngest dragons with the group walked through first. They, too, acted as vanguard, making sure no harm would come to their humans. A crowd waited for them.

Thirteen humans, and Arawn brought up the rear.

Renée gripped Rennin's hand. A chain reaction took place. D'Aubigné and Tyler, Aidan and Laurel, Ming and Jacques, and, surprisingly, Michelle and Sergio grasped hands. Only Hope seemed unafraid. The array of magical folk before them was enormous and varied.

As d'Aubigne had said, Fairies and Sprites were not the size of butterflies, but did have retractable wings; and Sprites proved to be a bit smaller than Fairies. Arawn whispered, sensing the dismay, "They can change size and grow needle-like teeth in battle. When Fairies or Sprites mate with Elves, Halflings form."

He pointed at Renée. "You have Halfling blood." To Laurel he said, "You have Fairy blood. All of you have some kind of Fey lineage."

Laurel spoke up. "Are angels here?"

"Oh, no!" Arawn said emphatically. "They, on occasion, visit, but angels are celestial beings. And to answer your unspoken question, none of us are immortal. Many live centuries, but we can die; even angels, although only an angel, which includes demons who are fallen angels, can kill another angel. Demons like to take possession of mortal beings and live vicariously through them. Angels manifest as human only when the need arises."

"How long have you been here?" Rennin asked.

"Two millennia."

"Wow!" said Aidan. His mind raced.

"Yes, I did." Arawn grinned. "I knew the one you call Jesus. He is the greatest of all celestial beings and gave all to help mankind."

"Is?"

"Yes. He has returned to the celestial realm. Humans crucified Him. He overcame that and returned to His realm. He will come back one day."

Rennin asked, "You called us *grandchildren* when you first appeared. How?"

"Ah, yes." Arawn walked through the crowd, stopping to speak or hold a baby.

"Politician," Laurel grunted under her breath to Aidan.

"Sh."

Arawn stopped and laughed loud and long. "Yes, my dear, I suppose I am. But I have been the leader here for fifteen hundred years. I am growing old. Soon I will take my place in the afterlife." He turned. "You can answer Rennin's question. You've seen it."

"I saw *what*, not *why*."

He nodded in a deferential way. "Correct. It must be seven hundred years now. I received a vision—one of your race, but with my blood, had to come in order to save them." He indicated Moonbeam and Filigree. "I ventured beyond and found a fair maiden to give my seed."

"Alexander O'Rourke," said Rennin. "His grandmother was the maiden."

The Elf King grinned broadly. "So, it worked. I see we still have dragons."

Arawn climbed onto a stage already standing in what must have been a town square. "Friends, family, Fey! Gather 'round." The throng pushed close.

"Now is the time to re-enter the world beyond." He proceeded to tell Earth's history, particularly as it pertained to those who had come to Faerie Keep with him that day. Then he pronounced, "We will not go all at once, and some may never go. But the portal is open. When these form a new governing body, we will be one world—one great council. But this eve we feast and become acquainted with our guests."

Potent wine, rich food, and hypnotic music soon flowed. Dancing and laughter made for merriment.

Rennin walked to a line of trees where a vast number of unicorns grazed. They were either sparkling white or inky black. He cocked his head to look intently at one white mare whose gold and silver entwined horn showed signs of yellowing, as teeth of a much older person. He said, "You look the way I've always envisioned Eunice."

The unicorn's laugh tinkled. "I *am* Eunice."

"The same from Draconis?"

"Yes. I found a portal in Morgan's Meadow. Arawn had opened it just for me, sensing I was the last of my kind there. He closed it upon my entrance. As you can see, I was not the last; but, like Arawn, I will die soon. Before I pass, I would so love to see Draco. If ever two such different species could have mated, I would have taken that dear one for life."

"Then, you must return to Draconis."

"I shall. And I'll end my time where I began." She shook her mane.

"I hope you live a while longer."

"Perhaps another hundred years, but no more."

"I'll take those years."

The feasting lasted well into the night. After breakfast of fruit and a thick porridge, Arawn took a large number of Fey of several varieties, along with his visitors and one unicorn, to Stonehenge.

Once back, the Elf King pointed a long, thin finger at Sabrina. "You, dear child, come."

She was able to walk through the barrier unscathed. She bowed to Arawn. "Rise," he said. "We will need lodging among your people. Arrange it and then go with these. There is a"—He looked at Laurel and squinted—"Navy flier that is meant for you."

"Stevens?" Laurel's voice rang out.

"Aye." Arawn nodded. "I believe he is called Stevens."

Without further ado, Arawn led his entourage to the locals who had come with Sabrina. She left him with her father and returned ready to leave with the healers. Instantly, the barrier fell, but the iris of the flower of life remained lit and shimmering in place.

"Wow!" Rennin muttered to his companions. "Talk about an abrupt personality that brooks no argument or nonsense."

Nods showed agreement.

Reporters swarmed past the group. Cameras flashed. Stories poured across the airwaves.

Fourteen people and one unicorn mounted six dragons, some of which were in a dither about Eunice, not having seen her in centuries, and left relatively unnoticed due to the fact that yet another realm had been revealed.

When the group got back to Alcatraz Island, they found the President waiting. First, he thanked them for all they had done. Then, he informed Rennin, as governor of Draconis, that a new United Nations would be forming.

The two leaders shook hands. Rennin said, "When you have specifics, let us know. We'll set up a way to communicate, and we'll send a delegation." He also informed the President that a delegation from Faerie Keep wanted to be included.

The President returned to the White House, stopping only long enough to touch a unicorn.

Rennin spoke with his group. "We'll be here a few more days. And we'll have extra people going back with us." He dipped his head toward d'Aubigne. "Set up that form of communication."

It took only moments to create a magical stream to carry voice patterns—something like a virtual phone. The only drawback is that for the time being it was only accessible from Alcatraz Island. The President would have to make another trip or find another way to relay information.

Sergio looked toward Michelle Zane once the mage had worked more magic. He leaned down and whispered to d'Aubigné, "Think you, Michelle, and I can go back now?"

"Why?"

"There's one more injection we need to try."

She stretched her eyes wide. "Zane?"

"Yes."

She rubbed her face. "But he's dead."

"Is he?"

"There was no curare in the bio-chem." She threaded fingers through her dark hair and pulled it back from her face. "If Michelle goes, so should Randall and Marshall. He's their father too."

"Works for me."

She nodded. "I'll round up everyone and get Filigree to take us back."

With no need for concealment, Filigree flew at a slower pace and viewed the renewed vegetation in areas that had been dead.

The young dragon intoned in a voice much like his father's, "Although thrice this world has engaged in war on a scale that involved all peoples, it has one more chance. I am uncertain if it will be afforded a fourth."

D'Aubigné caressed the dragon's head. "Let's hope we never have to find out." She took a deep breath and before long said, "We're home. Go directly to the precipice. Draco is waiting with Craig and Nicole."

Like a sentinel, Draco stood on the ledge. Filigree landed beside him. Randall, Marshall, and Michelle Zane, Caitlin and Morgan O'Rourke Zane, who was heavy with child, d'Aubigné O'Rourke Bishop, and Sergio Muñoz slid from his back.

Father and son dragons exchanged the traditional greeting. Then, Draco wrapped massive wings around his bonded human.

"It is so good to be home, wise one," d'Aubigné said.

"It's good to have you home." He glanced over his shoulder. "Craig had Zane placed in this tiny nook because it's the coldest place on Draconis. Filigree and I won't fit. Go and do this so Nicole can get on with life one way or another." He nudged the people forward with his nose.

Once inside, the arrivals found Craig leaning against the wall and Nicole lying beside her husband on a granite slab. Literal flakes of frost clung to the sparse hair on Harvey Zane's head.

Randall and Marshall lifted their mother away. "No!" she screamed. "Just let me die with him."

"Mom!" Michelle took her mother by the shoulders. "Let Sergio try to revive him."

"It's been too long." Nicole continued to weep.

"Maybe not. Craig has basically had him in a cryogenic chamber." Sergio took the older woman's hand. He looked into her eyes and realized Michelle was her spitting image. His heart gave a tiny lurch for fear of failing both of them. "Let me try, Mrs. Zane. What have you got to lose?"

"Please, Mom?" Michelle pled and turned big brown eyes to the doctor she was growing to care for on a deep level.

Nicole nodded with reluctance. She had a hard time denying the child, who evidenced the deep love between her and her husband, anything.

Sergio produced a filled syringe with a needle long enough to reach the heart.

D'Aubigné rubbed Nicole's arm. "I left some on Alcatraz Island, and the rest is in my pack with a preservation spell on it just in case we *ever* need it again." She nodded to Sergio. "Go ahead."

Sergio opened Zane's shirt, and with a hard thrust, jabbed the needle into the dead man's chest, injecting bio-chem antidote directly into Zane's heart muscle.

"Now what?" choked Nicole.

"We wait," Sergio whispered.

"Can we take him to the beach? He loves the beach. We often sit there and watch the sunset."

"I don't see why not."

Once on the shore, Casey Jamison joined her husband and daughter. She wrapped her arms around Nicole, her friend, and sat with her all night.

Morning came and Ming's children brought food. Nicole waved them away, though others took nourishment. "I have no appetite," the anxious woman murmured.

Still they waited. Draco laid his snout on Nicole's shoulder. She patted him. "I know you care. You're the only one who believed in me in the beginning. If this doesn't work, I want you to cremate him, and we'll spread his ashes here."

"It'll work," Michelle muttered.

"I hope so," echoed Sergio, placing his hand on Michelle's shoulder. She reached up and took it.

The sun began to sink. Nicole took Zane's hand. "I need you to watch the sunset with me." She turned toward Sergio. "His hand is warm."

The doctor strode toward the downed hero. As he reached Zane, the telltale seizure began, but Zane's thrashing was the worst any of them had seen.

Sergio pulled a device that looked like an EpiPen from a satchel he had brought with him.

"What's that?" Craig demanded.

"Midazolam."

"But he doesn't even have an I.V."

"Intramuscular."

"What?"

Their voices rose in volume. "No time to argue!" Sergio yelled and jammed the anti-seizure medication into Zane's thigh. Only seconds elapsed until the patient lay still but breathing shallowly.

Sergio said, "While you've been holed up in a virtual paradise, studies proved injection into the muscle worked faster than intravenous."

Both doctors sat back.

Hours later, a pearlaceous fingernail moon hung points down in the jet-black sky. Waves lapped soothingly onto Draconis's sandy shore. Harvey Zane's baritone croaked, "It's going to rain."

27

Sandy Shore

Nicole Zane screamed and gathered her husband in her arms. Their children added to a group hug.

Michelle disentangled from the pile and flung her arms around Sergio. "Thank you!"

He hugged her back. "Is there anyone else I can revive if this is payment?"

The young woman let go. "Sorry."

"Don't apologize."

Zane tried to sit up but lay back. "I feel weak." He gathered a handful of sand. "I love this sandy shore. Sorry I missed the sunset, darling." He took Nicole's hand.

She brought his hand to her cheek. "We have many more to catch."

Craig came forward. "Let's get you to a hospital bed for just a couple of days. I want to know what you experienced while you were gone—and you were *gone*."

"Yes, I was." He released a ragged breath. "I walked along a beach more beautiful than this one with a glowing man—Jesus. I asked if I was dead and He replied, 'Yes and no. Yes, but not permanently.' It confused me, but He told me if those he'd chosen accomplished their tasks, He'd send me back. If they failed, He'd take me through the gates of Heaven."

"So, it was like a kind of purgatory?" Craig asked.

"Only because I wanted closure—either home or Heaven. The waiting was the hard part, but He visited me every day. And in His presence, my anxiety ceased. I was never hungry or thirsty. I asked if everyone came to the beach to wait since I never saw anyone else."

Zane sighed. "He told me He placed those who had to wait somewhere they loved. I do love the beach. He refused to give me updates on what happened out here so as not to add to my worry. So, I contented myself to wait and commune with Him and bask in the sun."

Sergio interjected, "So, purgatory is a waiting place that you actually enjoy?"

Nicole sat flat on the sand with her legs extended. She lifted her husband's head to her lap.

"Oh, no." Zane shook his head, and rubbed his slick pate against the silk garment his wife wore. "First, there is a Hell. Those who practice evil with no conscience or inclination to change or repent do spend an eternity in a place of torment, even some people considered good, but we don't see the heart. Those who practice evil with some degree of question and have to wait do so totally alone in a place where they experience their greatest fear constantly. There really isn't a purgatory. Those who wait do so because they are not yet dead. I guess, it might be like a deep coma. And some on both camps—good versus evil—don't have to wait. They go directly to their everlasting reward or punishment."

Zane sat completely up with Nicole supporting him. "When you gave me the treatment, I suddenly had an overwhelming urge to swim. I went into the waves and felt as if I were drowning. Then, I woke up here."

"Amazing," said Craig. "Near death experiences recall light and dark. Casey saw both and had to make a choice."

"I suppose they would if they were only away for minutes. There was never darkness where I was. Also, time became irrelevant. Now, what's happened here?"

Draco nudged Zane and then picked him up. "Let's get you to the hospital before any more news."

They settled Zane and took turns telling all that had occurred.

"Demon blood, Elves, Fairies, Eunice *the* Unicorn?" Zane shook his head. "Shared and inherited memories? Cliff is truly Rennin's uncle? And Gerald has a woman?"

"Enough now," Craig said with authority. "My patient…"

Sergio cleared his throat.

Craig laughed. "*Our* patient needs nourishment and rest. So good to have you back, Zane."

The remainder of the Draconian contingency transferred to Puma Pass where Rennin revisited his home. Much to his dismay, the current National Football League commissioner found him. Rennin assured the man that West Coast teams could re-form and play could return to pre-war status.

By Lammas, celebrated August first, all Draconians prepared to go home. A few outsiders sought to go with them.

It came as no surprise Margaret Sanders intended to go with Cliff. And it was no big step to know Sam Mercier wished to make Draconis his home. Mary and the baby were still there.

A little more shocking was Arjun Ralston and Nidia Muñoz requesting to move to Draconis. However, considering Hope's gifts, it made sense. Nidia reminded Rennin that Sergio had no plans to return. "He's found where he belongs," she said. "I want my family to stay close."

Rennin turned to Arjun Ralston. "Are you in agreement?"

"Absolutely. We've been separated too long." He put his arm around Nidia. "And I've promised to make an honest woman of this terrific lady."

"Then, I'll welcome all of you. We'll be leaving tomorrow with a stop in Mom's Trading Post. There are a few loose ends there."

Sabrina Danaher approached Rennin. "Arawn said I was to go to Stevens."

Rennin took the young woman by the shoulders. "You've never even met him. How can you just decide to go to a man you don't know?"

"But I've dreamt of him my whole life. His name is Dale. No one has told me that." She described the lieutenant in detail. "I think you'll find he's dreamt of me also. In addition, although people no longer say I'm a lunatic, I don't fit here." She gave a little headshake.

He nodded. "Okay. You've made your arguments well."

The next day Rennin and company landed in Mom's Trading Post. Peter Pryor's entire family was packed and ready to go. Rennin laughed.

"And you'll all go as soon as we take care of some unfinished business here—starting at sunrise."

At the crack of dawn, Rennin, along with Bobby and Jennifer Willis, knocked resoundingly on the door to the home of Jennifer's parents, the Polsons. The once pleasant home had fallen into a state of disrepair. Paint flaked and shingles littered the yard, which was calf-high in grass dotted with dandelions and thistles.

In the few moments it took for a tired-looking, gray-haired man to open the door, Jennifer's past flashed across all three visitors' minds— her rape by James Wilburn, her possession which caused her to abduct Rennin's daughters to be sacrificed, her escape to Draconis. But the worst memory was the fact that her own mother had given her over to be used and abused.

The caramel-brown eyes of the aged man blinked as vague recognition kicked in. "Jenny?" he said, and repeated, "Jenny?"

He pushed the torn, squeaky screen open and stepped onto the porch. "Jenny?" he echoed once more. Then, he grabbed his daughter and pulled her into his arms. "Jenny, Jenny, Jenny," he sobbed. "I'm sorry. I'm so sorry. I didn't know what I was doing. I'm sorry."

"Dad," Jennifer said. "Explain."

Dwight Polson stepped back. "Your mother left me. She thought I spirited you away. Oh, how I wish I had! I have no clue where she is, and I don't care. I never want to see that bitch again. Once she was out of the house, it's like everything that happened became so clear. Before, it was like I wasn't in control of myself, like I was under a spell."

"You may well have been," Rennin said.

"When I realized what had really happened, I looked and looked for you, Jenny. I went to Bobby's folks."

Dwight looked around nervously. "You don't need to go there, Bobby. I knocked and knocked. I went back three days in a row. Finally, I got the authorities involved. When they broke the door down, they were both dead—a murder-suicide. The note was written in your mother's hand. She killed your father and then herself. The note said he had forced her to become pregnant, but when the baby was a boy, he had been angry and had abused both her and the child. I know for certain he was friends with my wife. I think he had tried to get a sacrifice and

205

failed." He took a deep breath. "The note did say she loved you and she was sorry."

Bobby let out a long sigh and rubbed his hands down his face. He put his arms around Jennifer. "I have no tears for them." Yet, he buried his face in her hair and she could feel the silent tears. She rubbed her spouse's arm in comfort.

"Can you ever forgive me?" asked Dwight.

"Yes, Dad," Jennifer said with a catch in her voice. "I know what it's like to be controlled by something."

"How are you? You're so beautiful, and you're still with Bobby."

"Married with kids." She took her father's hand and turned to Rennin. "Can we take him with us? Please?"

"If he wants to go." Rennin nodded.

"Yes!" Dwight said without hesitation. "What do I need to pack?"

"Nothing unless you want your own clothes and toiletries. If you have anything of personal value." Jennifer shrugged.

"Gypsy," Dwight said.

"Gypsy?" Jennifer cocked and eyebrow in question.

"My mutt. She wandered from house to house until I took her in. She was a gypsy."

Jennifer laughed. "By all means, bring Gypsy."

Rennin visited a few old friends—Padraig Riley and Travis Montague, who Rennin put in charge of all matters regarding O'Rourke Enterprises since Peter would no longer be there. With no use for money on Draconis, Rennin's instructions were for a small personal account for when the need arose to visit and for the rest of the profits above salaries and operation costs to go to various charitable organizations. No one else decided to leave their homes, so the morning brought loading the few belongings and people onto living aircraft. Only Dwight Polson hesitated at the actual sight of dragons. By the time they flew over the Caribbean, he was re-enacting Leonardo DiCaprio's "King of the World" from *Titanic*.

When they finally approached the sandy shores of Draconis, Draco greeted them with a blast of flames skyward as he waited in his usual spot atop the precipice.

Eunice neighed loudly from inside the protective talon cage in which Char carried her.

Draco jerked his head toward the sea and plunged in a free fall toward the beach. He landed and danced a little jig. "Eunice!" he roared and skipped back and forth across the sand.

Filigree flew out to meet them with a roll and a dive toward Moonbeam. She giggled a throaty dragon laugh.

"Why is she laughing?" asked Dwight.

Jennifer explained, "Filigree is Moonbeam's betrothed. There will soon be a dragon wedding."

"Ah. Love takes wing."

Jennifer scanned the beach and the friends below, then those on the backs of other dragons. "On more than one level, Dad." She took his hand. "Including father-daughter that we never got to have."

He brought her hand to his lips. "I do love you, baby."

28
Love Takes Wing

All dragons landed effortlessly on the immaculate beach. Draco charged toward his wife. The normal dragon hug lingered on each cheek. No question arose that love for each other bubbled through their veins.

The pearly dragon then greeted his fellow beasts with appropriate cheek touches before he scooped Eunice up and soared over the island. The unicorn laughed. "It's so good to be home. I've missed all of you."

"You must tell me all you've done."

"I found a mate. We had four offspring—three colts and one filly. Faerie Keep is a wondrous realm, but even there we've had to battle evil. Not all Fey are good. Those that lean toward vileness are Kelpie, Dracae, Selkie, Leanhaun, Goblin, and Leprechaun. Even those who practice in the light can become downright vicious if provoked. You've seen those tendencies even in the ones chosen to save Draconis. Think about it."

"Yes, I can see it, but they are very good people for the most part. I've had to temper d'Aubigné on occasion. She is extremely powerful—to the nth degree stronger than Quazel."

"Agreed. Now, what is this about an impending wedding? Moonbeam talked about your son all the way here. Your son! You finally had an egg, and he's so handsome."

Draco chuckled. "Filigree has been rather a handful. Char and Scarlet had Smoke almost right off. Sandy and Brindle had Sand Dollar a bit later. Sand Dollar wasn't very strong, but beautiful. Smoke adored her. Esmeralda and I had begun to think we'd never have offspring. Then our little golden bauble came. Twenty years later, Smoke and Sand Dollar had Moonbeam's egg. Sand Dollar passed with it though. Smoke has been father and mother to Moonbeam. Silver and gold. It just made sense. Esmeralda, Scarlet, and Sandy; Char, Brindle, and me: The offspring from Filigree and Moonbeam will have genes from the first six dragons born after the evil of Quazel. I've foreseen what the child will look like, but not the gender. The baby will be called Rainbow, and he or she will be the most powerful of our kind since the rebirth."

He set Eunice down in a field waving with fresh grain. A rustic-looking barn beneath two spreading oaks caught her eye. Draco said, "Your new home. I had it built when I found out you were coming."

She walked into the beautiful structure. "Settle in," Draco said. "Oh, and don't mention the little prophecy I just told you. I don't want the lovebirds to feel pressured."

He winged back toward the beach where humans new to the island were deciding where to go.

Michelle Zane insisted Sergio and his family—all six of them—were to come to the Zane home. Peter Pryor's brood went with Rennin to Isla Linda. Margaret Sanders, without hesitation, shared a home with Cliff and Laurel, and Dwight Polson moved in with his daughter.

Life slowly returned to normal, but with wedding plans in the works.

The first wedding slotted involved two long-awaited unions. In a joint ceremony, Clifton Spell and Margaret Sanders and Gerald McClarty and Stephanie Pitts exchanged wedding vows. Gerald and Stephanie honeymooned in the cave designated as the honeymoon suite, and Cliff and Margaret sailed out to sea for several days alone.

Then Arjun Ralston and Nidia Muñoz tied the knot. He had, after all, promised to make an honest woman of her. The happiest person in attendance was Hope. Having her parents together was a dream the little girl had never thought would come true. At the end of the reception, Michelle Zane fought to catch the bouquet, causing Laurel to scowl.

Sergio grinned and asked Michelle for an official date, beginning a whirlwind courtship with a wedding three months later.

When Dale Stevens met Sabrina Danaher the day she arrived on Draconis, his mouth dropped open on sight. He could hardly believe the shared dreams, but the two became inseparable. No doubt, the relationship would result in marriage.

All during the wedding frenzy, Aidan dropped by to do things with Laurel. They dated just as any young couple would and got to know each other on multiple levels.

Laurel asked pointedly, "Where is this leading us?"

Aidan laughed. "To a hand fasting."

"Hand fasting?"

"Basically, a Celtic wedding, but with all the other wedding craziness lately, I want to take a step back and give us time for something special. Besides, the next few weeks belong to Moonbeam and Filigree. We have to get them pounded and married."

Laurel soon discovered what a dragon wedding entailed.

Finalization of a new dragon home began two weeks before with the couple choosing a cleft in the sheer rock face filled with caves. Viewing the caves from the air showed a honeycomb-like structure. Many clefts were still unoccupied.

Moonbeam and Filigree explored several. Sitting on the precipice where Draco frequently stood sentinel, Filigree said, "I like the lowest one."

"Why?" Moonbeam asked.

"I like being able to stick my snout out and feel the spray from the crashing waves. The tide never gets that high, so flooding is not an issue."

She giggled. "I like it too, but I like the sandy floor rather than hard granite. It'll be warmer and softer. Okay. It's ours."

Residence chosen, the pounding began. The couple was fêted with gifts for it: woven mats to sleep on, jewels and gold and silver chains to adorn walls, even a wispy silk curtain to hang over the entrance. They were also given an allotment of food animals.

The day of the official joining arrived. As governor of the island, Rennin presided over the simple ceremony. The parents of the betrothed escorted them to the place of choice, which for Moonbeam and Filigree was the beach.

Rennin took a white silk cord and loosely looped it around the two dragons' snouts. "Although arranged many years ago by your parents, you have chosen to be bound," he said. "This is a commitment for life. If either of you wishes to back out, sever the cord."

Neither broke the symbolic bond. Rennin continued. "Then take this, your wedding cord, and place it above the entrance to your home. Go now and live as one."

The two dragons circled the island side-by-side, draped the cord above their cleft opening on a protruding stone, and returned to the beach. After hours of music, food, and dancing, they went to their home and barricaded themselves for two days.

"That's it?" asked Laurel.

"That's it," Aidan affirmed.

"Is that a hand fasting?"

"Not exactly, but, for certain, there is no dragon divorce."

"What about babies?"

"They will have one egg—someday."

"Only one? What if a mate dies?"

"You mean, will Smoke ever have another?" He shrugged. "I don't know. As for more than one baby—some stories tell of twins, but they're rare. It's said that Rose and Periwinkle were laid by the same mother and hatched at the same time. There are a few notations in old writings of siblings born centuries apart, but again rare."

"That's why there are so few," she said with sadness in her voice.

"That's also why they live so long."

With a sigh, she looped her arm around his. "Well, where does that leave us now?"

"I believe we have a ski date tomorrow." He kissed her nose and rejoined the party that was still in full swing.

"Ooh!" she mumbled and stomped after him.

29

Hoopla

*N*ext morning bundled in fleece-lined, seal-skin parkas and gloves, Aidan and Laurel hitched a ride from Periwinkle who had dropped by to visit her bonded twin. She dropped them at the top of the ski slope.

They strapped on old-fashioned waxed wooden skis and adjusted the ski poles to fit their height by turning the top to fit in notches on the bottom half. Laurel pulled down her goggles. Aidan touched her hand. "Hold on."

"Why? Afraid I'll finally beat you down?"

"Nope. I just wanted to tell you there's a special gift for you hidden on the trail. You have to find it."

"What is it?"

"A surprise, but you'll have to be very alert to spot it."

Her excitement bubbled. "How big is it?"

"Small." He kissed her and started down the leisurely slope.

"Unfair!" Laurel yelled and pushed off.

She stopped a few feet down. *Oh, if I race him, I'll miss the present. Ooh! Aidan O'Rourke, that's cheating. You know how competitive I am. I'll get even with you.*

Laurel looked back up the slope. *Did I miss it? Oh, I hope not.*

Then, she began a systematic descent. Back and forth across the etched trail she went, stopping every few feet and scanning her surroundings. She searched snowbanks, and low-hanging tree limbs. She looked in patches of brown scruffy grass.

Finally at the bottom, she spotted Aidan with a picnic waiting. She shook a ski pole at him. "Tell me it wasn't at the very top."

"It is no longer at the very top." He grinned.

"I didn't find anything."

"You didn't search hard enough."

"Aidan!"

"Oh, no." He wagged his head, one eye hooded. "You have to discover the surprise. Don't even think about hitting me with that pole."

Laurel threw the ski pole to the ground. As she did, she heard a metallic clink. "Oh, oh, oh! Sneaky snake!"

She dropped to her knees and twisted the top off the pole. She turned the pole up-side-down and all but throttled it. Out fell a ring.

Snatching it up, she stared at the two hands clasping a crown and forming a heart. The crown itself contained three diamonds.

"What is it?" she asked.

"A claddagh ring. It's sort of an Irish engagement ring. The hands are ours forming a heart. Stones can vary or be absent altogether. I chose the diamonds to make it more like a traditional engagement ring."

"Where and when did you get this?" She slipped the ring on.

"When we were in the U.K. Now, I guess the question is—Will you marry me?"

"Yes. But you lied to slow me down."

Aidan howled with laughter. "Yes, I did. Let's eat, and we can go back up and race down."

She snatched a sandwich, tucked skis under her arm, and began the trek back up the ski slope.

Aidan shook his head and rolled his eyes. *Love you to death, but you need lessons in romance.*

Atop the mountain again, the race was on. Aidan grinned as he held back and let Laurel get a big lead. Then he turned on the speed, passing her in the last stretch.

She screamed as he slid to a stop and showered her with snow. "You always win!"

"I've been doing this since I learned to walk. Your first time was about a year ago."

Both came out of their skis. Aidan caught Laurel around the waist and pulled her to him, her back to his chest. He kissed her neck just below her ear. "You need lessons in romance, Sunrise." He nibbled her ear lobe.

"Is that so, Island Boy?" She turned around into his embrace.

"Yes, indeed." His mouth found hers. Their tongues danced as the kiss deepened. Aidan ended with a soft bite to her lower lip.

Laurel shivered at the same time heat pooled in her groin.

Aidan put his forehead against hers. "I think we need a hand fasting very soon."

"Yeah. That'd be our wedding, right?"

"Yep."

"How soon?"

"Well, Imbolc, also known as Candlemas, is almost here. How about February second?"

"Okay, but why Groundhog Day?"

"It's mid-winter, a time for planning and hopes. In Celtic lore it's celebrated by fire and purification. In Christian belief, it's forty days after the Nativity and a purification ceremony."

"Fire? I won't have to walk on hot coals, will I?"

"No, silly, but the colors are red, orange, and white. You'll look like a brilliant sunrise."

"Works for me then."

"Let's get home before Uncle Cliff demands a shotgun wedding."

Moonbeam and Filigree emerged from their solitude. They flew around the island twice. Moonbeam giggled. "Aidan gave Laurel the ring."

"I know. She's in a dither—what to wear and all that." Filigree chortled. "I'm glad we have scales."

"And such magnificent scales you have."

"Ah, my silver sliver, you are the beauty."

"Say silver sliver ten times without messing up." Moonbeam snickered. "Let's see what's happening with the wedding plans."

They swooped onto the shore of Isla Linda where the O'Rourke women had Aidan corralled on a stepstool. They measured and made notations.

"So, what are you wearing?" asked Moonbeam with her dragon grin in place.

"I wish I could wear my birthday suit like you," Aidan griped. "This is a pain in the ass."

"Shut up," said Renée, Aidan's mother, "or I'll give you a pain in the ass with a straight pin."

Aidan's bonded dragon batted lashes that could have been tiny twigs. "Actually, I didn't wear my birthday suit. I've molted a number of times."

"Ha, ha!"

Around a few pins held between tight lips, Renée said, "He's wearing a Balmoral kilt in O'Rourke tartan, orange, red, and black. He'll have that 1980s rock-star hair pulled back in a sash of same tartan. The kilt pouch will have our motto, 'Serviendo guberno,' ('I govern by serving,') embroidered on it. The only concession I'm making is letting him go barefoot for the ceremony at sunrise on Imbolc on the beach."

"On the big island?" Filigree asked.

"Yes, since that's where his 'Sunrise' washed ashore." Renée rolled her eyes.

"Okay," said Moonbeam with a snigger. "I think we'll see how the bride is coming. Do you have music?"

"Would you get Nicole on that for me?" asked Aidan.

"Love to. And I'll get Casey on food."

"You're a lifesaver."

The dragon duo flew off. "Were we *that* silly?" asked Filigree.

"Almost," said Moonbeam. "But that's okay. Love can be silly."

The newlywed dragons landed at Cliff's home in Sierra Bluff where Laurel was undergoing the same treatment at the hands of Ming and Margaret as Aidan was with the females in his family.

"Ow!" Laurel squealed as Ming poked her with a pin.

"Lovely," said Moonbeam.

"Is it too late for Aidan and me to elope to the States, Filigree?" Laurel asked, irritation oozing.

The golden dragon laughed. "Afraid so."

"I like the dress very much," said Moonbeam.

"Off the shoulders shows my freckles," Laurel complained.

"Your hair will cover your shoulders." Moonbeam offered encouragement with emphatic head bobbing. "And since it fits your figure so well, nobody would notice a little freckle."

"You think white washes me out?"

"You look beautiful, Laurel," Filigree said. "Is that lace over satin?"

Laurel lifted one arm and the long, flared sleeve hung to her ankles. "Yes. Hm. Too bad human men don't notice such detail."

215

"Some do. Aidan does."

The bride-to-be pointed to the neckline. "Are rubies appropriate?"

"It fits the color scheme," Margaret groused. "I'm beginning to wish you'd elope too."

Ming held up the plaid sash that matched Aidan's kilt.

"Hm," mused Filigree. "Do you know what Aidan's wearing?"

"No!" Margaret and Ming snapped in unison.

Ming pointed a sharp finger. "And don't you tell her!"

"Okay, okay. I just hope Aidan doesn't have to use the knife in the pouch." He grabbed Moonbeam's wing and they soared away.

"Pouch?" yelled Laurel. "Is he only covering his manhood?"

"I'll get you for that!" Ming screeched.

Both dragons laughed so hard they could hardly fly. Moonbeam eked out, "That was mean." She sucked in breaths. "But funny."

"She *is* pretty. The hair wreath of miniature red rosebuds and baby's breath will be lovely."

"And the bouquet of the same with shamrocks for luck."

"I just hope they don't try to sneak off to wed. There would be hell to pay."

"Yeah, but the hoopla is driving them nuts."

Filigree wiggled the ridge above his eyes like a mischievous brow. "Wait until the wedding night rigmarole."

They laughed again.

Finally, sunrise on February second arrived. Every resident of Draconis turned out for the future governor's wedding. They sat in concentric circles. Dragons formed the outermost ring.

A small disturbance of air caught the guests' attention. Through a shimmering veil walked Arawn and his two daughters. Dressed in a formal kilt, Rennin, who already stood at the center of the circle, cocked an eyebrow.

The Elf King approached. "We are not too late?"

"No," Rennin assured. "The bride and groom have yet to arrive."

"Good then." Arawn held out an intricately crafted brass wedding bell. "For their home." He grinned. "From what I witnessed of their temperaments, one or the other might need to summon help."

Rennin accepted the gift on the couple's behalf. "They can place it on a shelf beside the door to the house just finished near the grotto in the center of Isla Linda. Many thanks."

The Elves bowed their heads and took a place among the family.

Well, just insinuate yourselves. I don't think I want to argue with you. Rennin surveyed where the veil had appeared. *He could have done that hundreds of years ago and stopped all the bad things that happened, but he let mankind battle his own wars. He could have stopped Quazel rather than planting his seed so that a savior would be born. Nope.* He shook his head. *That's one battle I choose to leave alone. He can come and go as he pleases.*

Two shadows loomed above just as the sun peeked above the horizon. Moonbeam set Aidan and Filigree set Laurel down in front of Rennin and then took places with the dragons.

Behind Rennin as the couple landed, bagpipes heralded their arrival with a stirring rendition of "Ode to Joy." Standing back-to-back, as soon as the music stopped, Aidan and Laurel turned slowly three hundred sixty degrees, forming a Cain as they scattered the same herbs d'Aubigné had used in the Merkaba to form a circle around them. As they turned, they chanted:

> *The Mighty Thee,*
> *My protection be.*
> *Encircle me.*
> *You are around*
> *My life, my love, my home.*
> *Encircle me,*
> *O, sacred Thee.*
> *The Mighty Thee.*

The couple faced Rennin who presided over the ceremony. A Céllidh band, made up of an Irish harp, flute, tin whistle, and bedhráh played "This Is My Father's World" before Rennin spoke.

"From ancient times a circle has symbolized unity. It has no beginning, no end. You have formed a circle today. You stand at its center. Is it your desire to unite as one?"

Together they said, "It is."

Rennin opened his hand. In his palm lay two chains linked to from rings. "Hundreds of years ago, my ancestor, Aidan O'Rourke, who came to Draconis to break an evil curse, created two loops from a chain of a watch. He gave them to his son, Rennin, on the day he wed Morgan Fitzpatrick. Rennin inherited the watch and created more rings. One set he gave to his son, Cameron, from whom I descended, from whom the Aidan before you now descended. These are that set. They have been worn by an O'Rourke couple since the day Cameron married Holly Montague, also known as Holehah of the Iroquois tribe. Renée and I wore them until this morning. As is tradition, I give them to you, my son."

Aidan took the rings. Rennin said, "I would ask you to place them on each other's fingers, and I would ask you, Aidan, to recite the words that you've heard many times, the words associated with these rings."

Aidan pulled Laurel's claddagh ring from her left hand and placed it on her right. Then he put the wedding loop on her hand saying, "'Heart of my heart, life of my life, you are my reason for breathing; and I will love you until the day I die.'"

Laurel put the other loop on Aidan and worked her mouth, but no words came out. Aidan kissed her hand.

Rennin said, "No words are necessary. Your actions have spoken."

He then produced a braided cord in red, orange, and black. He asked, "Please join right hands."

Aidan and Laurel clasped hands as if in a firm handshake. Holding one end of the cord, Rennin looped the braid around the couple's hands.

"Hand fasting dates back centuries. It spans several cultures. In the Scottish Highlands, it once served as a temporary binding to determine compatibility. After a year and a day, the couple could dissolve the union—if there were no children—or agree to remain joined. In other societies, it was a complete binding. Sometimes it served as a common law commitment. Often it has been used when neither clergy nor magistrate was available, and on occasion, only the bride and groom with no witnesses used hand fasting."

As he spoke, he looped the long cord around Aidan's and Laurel's hands. "In the end, the common denominator is the agreement to be bound." He pulled both ends together and tied a square knot. "Thus, the phrase, 'tie the knot.'"

Rennin placed his left hand on top of the couple's bound hands and his right on the bottom. "On Draconis, we use hand fasting and/or rings to signify a lasting union." He looked into Laurel's dark brown eyes. "Laurel Elaine Moss, do you agree to be bound to Aidan Alexander O'Rourke and to never break the tie until death parts you?"

"I do," she said with confidence.

He turned to his son and stared into matching emerald orbs. "Aidan Alexander O'Rourke"—Rennin's mind went back to his vision quest in the Himalayas and seeing a blond-haired baby in his mind's eye, and then to Aidan's birth and realizing he had had a premonition of his son. The thoughts took only seconds, but the rest of his request came out through stifled tears as he realized his youngest child had become a man—"Do you agree to be bound to Laurel Elaine Moss and to never break the tie until death parts you?"

Aidan grinned. "I do."

"Blessed be the tie that binds. As is our custom and law, I declare you husband and wife. You may kiss to seal the commitment."

The two young people leaned in and kissed in a socially appropriate gesture.

They withdrew their hands from the fasting cord. Rennin held it up. "This is a symbol to adorn your front door. Let the feasting begin."

As Rennin had said, Aidan and Laurel's wedding feast was bounteous; the music, pert; the dancing, lively; the energy, contagious. Over a glass of nectar wine, Draconis's very potent fermented beverage, Gerald whispered to Rennin. Rennin stepped back laughing. "You're kidding me!"

Gerald shook his head. Rennin grasped his hand and slapped his back. "Well, congratulations, Daddy!"

Gerald grinned. "You know, Stephanie is younger than you, but this will still be her only child."

"It's great. Really."

"We've already decided on a name, no matter what gender."

"Do tell."

"Ruairc."

"The ancient pronunciation of O'Rourke. I'm honored."

Cat calls began as single ladies lined up for the bouquet toss. Laurel threw over her head with a hard thrust without looking. The flowers landed in the hands of Dale Stevens.

Female shouts of, "Unfair," and, "Do over," resounded.

"Not on your life!" Dale hollered. "I caught this fair and square and without even trying. Sabrina!" he called into the crowd of girls. "Will you marry me?"

"Yes!" she squealed.

Aidan put his arms around Laurel. "That worked out well."

"Yep."

A small ruckus caught their attention as Moonbeam and Filigree argued about which one of them should transport the newlyweds to the honeymoon suite.

Rose whispered to Draco who nodded. Over the din, he roared, "I have the solution. As her first official act of flying since sprouting her wings, Rose's daughter, Dandelion, will fly Aidan and Laurel to their destination." All eyes turned toward the very young butter-yellow dragon as she bounced up and down.

That's what you get for fighting, Aidan sent to Moonbeam's mind.

Right, "Island Boy." I can't wait to witness your first one. "Sunrise" might go super nova.

Aidan laughed before he and Laurel climbed onto Dandelion.

"Ready?" the dragon said.

"Yes," the couple answered, and they were off.

She let them down onto the landing outside the honeymoon suite. "Smooth ride, Dandelion," Aidan said. "Thanks."

"Welcome. 'Bye now." She winged away.

Aidan scooped Laurel up and carried her into the special place for newlyweds. Rose oil burned in clay pots over candles, and rose petals covered the satin-sheeted bed. A banner over the headboard bore the Moss motto: *En la rose je fluerie.* (I flourish in the rose.)

He set her on the bed.

"My, my. How romantic," he said.

"Yes." She bit her knuckle. "I thought you were of Irish descent. Do they wear kilts too?"

"Yes, ma'am."

"Hm. So, what does an Irishman wear under his kilt?"

"Would you like me to show you?"

"Huh-huh."

Aidan flipped his kilt up.

Laurel's eyes stretched wide.

Aidan grinned.

"I like what you have on, Island Boy."

Kneeling in front of her, he slid his hands beneath her dress and up her legs. "The native strives to please."

Epilogue

The message came via old-fashioned light-emitted Morse code. The One World Council set its first meeting. Representatives from around Earth, from Faerie Keep, and from Draconis scheduled to meet a month after Aidan O'Rourke's wedding. Since dragons were to be included, Alcatraz Island was designated One World Headquarters. Meetings were to take place in spring and fall with called meetings in case of emergency.

Draco stood on the precipice on Draconis and looked out over the sapphire blue ocean. D'Aubigné O'Rourke Bishop sat on his back.

"There's nothing to be afraid of," Rennin O'Rourke said from the back of Smoke on Draco's left.

"We're here with you always," Char intoned in his gravelly voice from his friend's right with Clifton Spell nestled against his scales.

"I'm not afraid. I'm excited," Draco informed.

Three magnificent beasts took flight with their special passengers flush against their necks.

Some hours later, Smoke and Char landed on Alcatraz Island. Representatives from around the world had seen them. They were no surprise.

Draco circled in a slow descending spiral. Humans shielded their eyes as the light reflected from his gleaming white scales.

At last, Draco put down between his friends. He leaned his head back and let loose a burst of flame skyward as he roared, "The meeting may come to order. Let us *never* forget that we are *one world*."

The End
Or is it…

The Beginning?

July 31, 2013

Word Count—54,309

Ode to a Dragon

I

You fill the mind with mystery and lore.
Some say you existed in days of yore.
I can't be sure. I was not there before
The stories were changed, embellished; therefore,
Creating beast, monster, god of war.

II

'Tis a pity to have killed such a thing.
To see you, touch you would make my heart sing.
Your accolades and terrors still do ring,
Your praises and threats of massive spread wing,
Making you a lord, a master, a king.

III

For most today you are no more than myth.
For those who believe, our spirits are kith.
What you were fills imagination's fifth.
Bards' words sung: hard scales. Stronger still your pith—
Your majesty, might, the awe you fought with.

IV

Legend tells us that your downfall was greed.
Your desire for gain planted evil seed.
You became a scourge that made man to bleed,
It was your thirst for glory that, indeed,
Unleashed your power, your fury, your need.

V

As Satan you are described in Scripture.
Such a horror past? What will be your future?
The Bible places in the heart mixture,
And in mind paints quite a bleak picture,
Imprint of malice, of dread, of fissure.

VI

Could a creature so splendid be cruel?
Must you with all mankind strive and duel?
Pagan and pious feed fire with fuel
Of your menacing, dominant, hard rule—
Perhaps a treasure, a gem, a jewel.

VII

That you were misjudged I pray in my heart.
Your mystique caused awe from the very start.
My line finds not you to pierce like a dart,
Or person or character to be tart.
This I see for my piece, my say, my part.

VIII

You are a Celtic guardian, a godsend.
The foes of comrades you surely could rend.
For an ally you might fight and defend;
A Celt sustain, uphold, and help to mend
As if a father, a brother, a friend.

IX

The Chinese paint you as a glowing sight;
Respect and honor your power and might.
You manifest fantastical and bright,
Shining, piercing the deep darkness of night
As a vision, a protector, a light.

X

For some you are a conquering hero.
Even now, your praise they sing and bestow.
The fire in your eyes, your mouth all aglow
Make respect in the hearts of men to show
Whether you be a fiend, a friend, a foe.

XI

Me? I believe you are a champion,
Perhaps, even angel and companion.
In my honest, but humble, opinion
To influence you need not a minion
To assert control, sway, dominion.

XII

You are magical I choose to believe.
In no way would you me trick or deceive.
Contrarily, what you did was to leave
Within desire your knowledge to achieve,
Your wisdom to take, accept, and receive.

XIII

You now know the doctrine which I do choose.
You have been my inspiration, my muse.
Now invisible, none can you accuse
Of having influence upon my views.
Neither me coerce, me force, me abuse.

XIV

This word scripted, I hope all will agree:
You are by far something I wish to see.
My heart knows honest and good you would be,
Not evil, dealing underhandedly;
Nay, no doubt, you are strong and proud and free.

XV

Until such a time as this should occur,
All you can be to my mind is a blur.
Still it would seem that all men can concur
Without any fleeting conscience or err
Fanciful thoughts you cause, you make, you stir.

XVI

I shall sleep tonight; dream of you, perchance.
My heart will leap for joy; my spirit dance.
In all you would never leave me to chance
My soul with your strength and powerful stance
You would endow, would imbue, would enhance.

XVII

Magical enigma you ever don!
Mystery last eon after eon!
May your fantasy linger on and on,
And wistful thoughts of you never be gone,
My sentinel, my watchman, my dragon!

A short-list finalist at the Faulkner Wisdom Competition

About the Author

*L*ike many of her characters, Janet is a history buff and loves anything of historical significance from old cars to old cemeteries. Get to know Janet and you'll see why she's been critically acclaimed at the Faulkner Wisdom Competition and why her writing continues to receive 4- and 5-star reviews. Her novel, *Spirits' Desire*, the second book in her *Legend of Draconis* series, won The Critter's, Preditor's and Editor's Award while the third book in *The Raiford Chronicles*, *Broken*, was a short-list finalist (top 20) at the Faulkner Competition. It could be that readers see so much of her in her characters: mother, educator, author, editor, and a person who has overcome great obstacles and still holds on to her faith.

http://www.janettaylorperry.com/

http://janettaylor-perry.blogspot.com/

https://authorcentral.amazon.com/gp/profile

https://www.facebook.com/Author-Janet-Taylor-Perry-299698950061301/

janettaylorperry@gmail.com

https://www.facebook.com/janettaylorperrybooks/

Instagram: @janettaylorperry & @jtaylorperry

Twitter: Janet Taylor-Perry— @mom5kidz421

Goodreads: https://www.goodreads.com/author/show/7376480Janet_Taylor_Perry

Pinterest: https://www.pinterest.com/mumzy25/

YouTube: https://bit.ly/30hJsYg

Janettaylorperry.com—For a reading experience
EXTRAORDINAIRE!

www.ingramcontent.com/pod-product-compliance
Lightning Source LLC
Chambersburg PA
CBHW020327200626
46814CB00006BB/2444